STORIES OF JERUSALEM, ISRAEL AND OTHER LOVES

Stories of Jerusalem, Israel and Other Loves

iUniverse books may be ordered through booksellers or by contacting:

iUniverse
1663 Liberty Drive
Bloomington, IN 47403
www.iuniverse.com
1-800-Authors (1-800-288-4677)

ISBN: 978-1-4759-7347-1 (sc)
ISBN: 978-1-4759-7349-5 (hc)
ISBN: 978-1-4759-7348-8 (ebk)

Library of Congress Control Number: 2013901869

Printed in the United States of America

iUniverse rev. date: 03/01/2013

Contents

AMERICA

Dedication

To our lovely and talented granddaughters, Elise, Adina, Talia, and Jenna, who are very different from each other but, nonetheless, take after me.

Introduction

"Are these true stories?" You ask.

"Are all brides beautiful?" I retort.

Many brides are beautiful. Many brides are beautiful but not altogether beautiful and a few are not but, perhaps, could have been beautiful.

So it is with regard to truth in the Jerusalem, Israel stories.

Some are true: **My Hard-earned Small Change**, **Bus Rambles**, **Our First *Tu B'Shvat* in Israel**, **The *Shuk***, **Our Post Office in Jerusalem**, **A Family Visit** and **Souvenirs.**

Some are true but not altogether true: **Jerusalem Bus Ride**, **Potato Chips**, **The Newspaper Subscription**, **Challenge**, and **The Jerusalem Volunteer Police Force**,

The rest are not true but could have been true. Each has an element of truth. **The Storm Eased** was inspired by a dear friend, Roz Yunker. It is not true but it is in character. She was that kind of person. *Shahid* and **The Reporter** were inspired by newspaper articles in <u>The Jerusalem Post</u>. The story in **The Experiment** is not true but the experiment, itself, is true. The Israeli government built homes for middle and upper middle class families in a depressed neighborhood in order to mix populations and upgrade the neighborhood.

The **Irene** stories were inspired by stories told to me by Irene Danzicer, a dear friend and amazing person.

The last series of stories are my family's legacy: **America I, II, and III** were told to me and I believe them to be true. The stories in which I am an active participant are true. Especially true in **My Wedding Gown** is that the hem went up and down and the seams went in and out.

We, my husband, Hans Benjamin Marx, and I lived in Jerusalem, Israel for seventeen years. We arrived during the summer of 1994 just after President of the United States, Bill Clinton, Prime Minister of Israel, Yitzhak Rabin, and Chairman of the Palestine Liberation Organization, Yasser Arafat, signed a peace agreement on the lawn of the White House.

All of Israel was euphoric. "Is it possible to live in peace with our enemies?"

"Really, is it possible?"

We heard the question over and over again. People hoped with all of their hearts that it would be true. The Israelis wanted peace for their generation and for all of the following generations.

The peace agreement did not last long. Bombs blew up bus shelters, buses, and restaurants. Sometimes bombs went off at the same time in different parts of the country. Suicide bombers blew themselves up in order to make more efficient the mass murder of innocents.

The euphoria which had greeted us when we had arrived in Israel was replaced by grief, fear, and anger. As difficult as life was to become in Israel, the country persevered. Individuals found themselves and others capable of acts of strength, courage, and kindness which they would not have known existed.

For over ten years of the time we lived in Jerusalem, I was a member of David Brauner's writers' group. During that time I wrote over one hundred stories. A sample of those stories makes up this book.

We left Israel for the United States in 2011. Much of Jerusalem, Israel had become a part of me. I like to feel that I left something good of myself in Jerusalem.

JERUSALEM, ISRAEL

My Hard-Earned Small Change

"Twenty-four shekels and forty agorot for the cab fare? I'll round it up to twenty-five shekels to include a tip. No problem."

My change purse was full and I had no difficulty collecting the exact change. No problem having exact change for the return trip, either, I noted happily. I paid the cab driver and we went our separate ways, satisfied.

Had I not had the exact amount of money and would have given the driver, let's say, thirty shekels and asked for five shekels change, he could very well have said, simply, with a little smile, as other drivers have before him, "I don't have change," proceeding to pocket the entire amount.

"You don't have a five shekel piece or five single shekels?" I would ask incredulously. I would receive a blank look in return. The money would stay in his pocket.

That moment would require an immediate examination of my options. For one, I could put my hand into his pocket and retrieve the money. Forget that. An Israeli taxi driver? That would be asking for real trouble.

Other than that, I could have called him a thief and he would have looked at me as if I had lost my mind and the money would stay pocketed. Or I could have given him a very nasty look and, of course, the money would still stay pocketed. The result would be the same. I would leave the cab feeling like I'd "been had," a *freier*, a sucker.

In Israel there is nothing worse than being a freier. Lesson #1 at the introductory session for new *olim*, immigrants: "Never, ever be called a freier! Anything but that."

The trick, I learned quickly was to always have enough small change in my purse so that I could feel comfortable ordering or hailing a cab any time I would wish knowing that I would have sufficient change to pay the exact fare.

Seems easy enough? Easier said than done. For the days in which I felt a need to fill my change purse I would go to the green grocer and buy, let's say, two oranges and four apples. The cost, I would estimate, would be less than ten shekels. I would offer the shop keeper a one hundred shekel bill and wait for all the gorgeous change to appear.

"You don't have anything smaller?"

I would root around in my change purse. "Fifty shekels?" I offered.

"Smaller."

Reluctantly I wold put ten shekels on the counter. Three shekels and a few agorot appeared in exchange. Not much of a bonanza in small change.

OK, how about the bakery? I plunked down a one hundred shekel bill for warm, cheesy *burekas* just out of the oven. The same story.

"Don't you have anything smaller?"

I would end up with two shekels and twenty agorot change.

The post office! I would buy postage stamps. The post office had to have an abundance of small change. It was a government institution, for heaven's sake! Who makes the money? The government does of course. It was a 'no-brainer'. At least that is what I thought. Was I surprised?!

Again I ended up with fewer than five shekels in change. The clerk said that if I did not have something smaller he would have to go to the back room where the change was stored. I did not have the patience to wait. He won.

That's when I learned that an epidemic of insufficient small change plagued the entire city of Jerusalem.

I did, eventually, find a dependable way to accumulate small change. And that was at the *shuk*, the open market. I had not a clue to why they always had small change when the rest of the city did not but that's the way it was. I planned my attack.

I would buy thirty shekels of fresh fish and give the vendor a one hundred shekel bill. No problem. I would receive seventy shekels back. Another one hundred shekels for smelly cheese. More than fifty shekels back. Another one hundred shekels broken at the dried fruits and nuts stall. Fifty shekels each at different vendors for carrots, peppers, and strawberries. When I was finished, I would count several twenty shekel bills and coins of all kinds, too numerous to bother counting. My change purse was full.

Ho, ha! I could take a cab to any destination in Jerusalem at any time for several days to come. I had as much change as I needed.

Still, one must be on one's toes, so to speak, or all the cockiness and the little bit of arrogance earned at the shuk could easily be deflated a notch or two.

For instance, yesterday, when I was on the way to city hall, I noticed a young woman accosting people as they walked by. She stopped one after the other without success. She saw me, and with a forced smile, came over.

"I'm sorry to bother you but I have a serious problem. I parked my car over there." She pointed. "But I don't have enough change for the meter. Would you mind changing a 100 shekel bill for me? I'm sorry but I don't have anything smaller." She was pleading.

I groaned. I had been to the *shuk* that very morning and my purse was full. Reluctantly I pulled it from the depths of my being and slowly counted enough small change to equal one hundred shekels.

"Thank you so much." The worried look on the woman's face disappeared and was replaced by a broad smile.

"I was becoming desperate. Nobody else had change. I can't thank you enough." The stranger practically ran towards the meter next to her car. The Meter Maid was in sight and, with her pad for giving tickets in her hand, she was checking.

I should have felt good as I usually do when I help someone. After all, what are we here for?

I had such a successful morning at the shuk. What did I do? I gave this stranger practically all of my hard-earned small change. The satisfaction I had felt at having done a good deed dissipated. Suddenly, again, I felt like a freier.

Bus Rambles

The bus driver's head drooped, his chin almost touching the steering wheel.

"You should be ashamed of yourself. A healthy young man like you! I'm only an old lady. I'm not only old enough to be your *Ima*, your mother, I'm old enough to be your *Savta*, your grandmother. Is this the way you treat your Savta? Shame on you! Shame on you! A hundred times, shame on you!"

The rest of the bus sat quietly. They were not involved. Their consciences were clear. This was between the driver and the little old lady sitting behind him.

The little old lady was very old, very little, and bent. When she had boarded the bus at the shuk she was carrying two full shopping bags, each weighing more than she did. Laboriously, she tossed first one bag onto the bus and then the other. Then she climbed aboard. The young woman sitting up front gave her her seat. The seats closest to the driver were reserved for the elderly and/or infirm. The little old lady sat down, arranging her shopping bags around her.

"I live on Herzl Road number 86. Stop in front."

"I can't stop there. There's no bus stop."

"All of the drivers stop there. They all know me."

"I only stop at bus stops. I can't stop anywhere else."

"What are you? New? You don't know? You have no heart? No soul? Maybe you know but you don't understand. You have to stop by my house. How can I carry two big bags like these two streets from the bus stop? You see how heavy they are. Everybody stops. You have to stop, too."

The driver did not answer. He knew what he had to do.

The little old lady continued. She screeched at the driver, reaching ever higher pitches. When the driver passed her home her voice reached a crescendo. Some riders put their fingers in their ears.

Dead silence followed when the bus stopped as scheduled and the little old lady descended the steps, slowly and carefully, pushing her bags in front of her.

The driver's head rose from the wheel.

The silence, however, did not last. The man who had sat next to the little old lady offered his opinion.

"You should have left her off in front of her house. She was just a little old lady. What's it to you or anybody here if you make an extra stop?"

The woman sitting up front on the other side of the bus had another opinion

"What do you mean, an extra stop? His job is to stop at bus stops. Who told her to buy so much? Next time she'll find fewer bargains."

Another voice rang out. "Once in a while, you can make an exception. Nobody is going to get killed if you make an extra stop. You saw what she looked like."

"I stop only at bus stops. You want I should lose my job?" The driver's head drooped again.

"Lose your job? To let a little old lady off, you're going to lose your job? This is Israel. In Israel you don't lose your job to let an old lady off."

Yes, this is Israel. Where else would we be?

The man who told the driver that in Israel a driver does not lose his job for an act of kindness was Israeli. What else would he be?

At another time, with another driver, a young blind girl traveling alone, boarded the bus.

"I am going to Pisgat Ze'ev." She told the driver.

"Pisgat Ze'ev? You're on the wrong bus. That's in the opposite direction. You have to go across the street and take the bus going the other way."

The young blind girl turned around and descended.

The driver cut the engine and stepped down from the bus after the girl.

"Wait here." He told the blind girl.

He stood by the open door to consider the passersby on the busy street. Finally he stopped an older woman who did not appear to be in a hurry.

"This girl has to take the bus on the other side. You see the bus stop across the street? That's where she has to go. Take her across the street and make sure that she takes the right bus."

The woman nodded and took the blind girl's hand.

"You look just like my Surele. She'll be sixteen tomorrow and I want to buy her a present but I don't know what . . ."

Together they crossed the street.

The driver re-boarded and the bus was on its way once more. He was not worried about losing his job. Nobody complained.

A strapping young Arab boy was sitting up front on a crowded bus when an elderly woman, badly crippled, boarded. She stopped before his seat and stared at him. He folded his arms across his chest, looked straight ahead, and smiled. He made no attempt to move.

"Give her your seat. Now!" The driver spoke gruffly to the young man in Arabic.

The young boy jumped up and walked to the back of the bus.

The crippled woman thanked the driver and sat down in the young boy's place.

Passengers, also, were kind. A young girl boarded a bus to go to school, took a seat, searched her pockets and started to cry.

"What is the matter?" Asked the passenger sitting next to her as if everything was her business.

"I left my money home. I have no money for school."

The passenger opened her purse. Other passengers contributed. A collection was made. Without another word, the young girl had the money she needed. There was no problem. In a country of Jewish mothers and Jewish fathers this was not a problem.

When we were new to the country, we were given an address in Jerusalem with scant instructions about how to go there. We boarded the bus we were advised to take, sat down, and took out the paper with the address on it. We held it between us and tried to decipher it.

"Let me see your paper." Our neighboring passenger took the address out of our hands, looked at it and scratched his head.

"Who is going to Herzog Street number 4?" he asked loudly.

"I am," answered an elderly woman with a big smile on her face. "I pass it on the way to my granddaughter. I'll take them there. No problem."

Each time the bus stopped for the next three stops we heard, "No, not this one. Two more stops or maybe another stop and we will be there."

Finally, our fellow passenger and we descended together and we were accompanied to the door of our destination.

Of course, there is occasional unkindness and thoughtlessness from both drivers and passengers. It happens. People are people. They could be in bad moods or just plain tired.

Yet, there is a difference.

You may call it prejudice if you wish.

Our First *Tu B'Shvat* in Israel

"We are going to plant trees!" Dorit, our teacher, smiling proudly, searched each of our faces for the enthusiasm she hoped to share.

"It will be *Tu B'Shvat*, the holiday of The New Year of the Trees. Besides eating fruit, nuts and other good things, we also plant trees. The trees will grow and flourish not only for us but also for our children and grandchildren. We will be doing a *mitzvah*, performing a good deed."

We were a motley crew of immigrants newly arrived from several countries who were privileged to attend a government subsidized *ulpan* class where we were given the opportunity to learn Hebrew and, also, to become acculturated to Israel, our newly adopted country.

Did we share Dorit's enthusiasm? Some of us, certainly. Were we curious? Wary? Skeptical? Sure. But this promised to be a new experience and one heavily subsidized by the government. We were all game.

I would have loved to say that the appointed day dawned bright and clear as an early spring day often does. It did not. Actually it dawned gray and damp as an early spring day also does from time to time. I did say that our class was subsidized, didn't I? Did I mention that the cost to each of us was miniscule? Were we going to miss an opportunity to learn and share in the customs of Israel? Would we let a 'freebie' go by? Not if we could help it.

Dorit was waiting for us as she said she would. We all came. Everybody, that is, but Vladimir, one of our fellow students who had come from Russia.

"No matter," Dorit told us. "We are not about to wait. If Vladimir, for whatever reason, misses a golden opportunity, we will have to tell him about it afterwards."

The bus was late. We took it in stride. We had all come dressed for the weather and with a little hopping up and down or side to side we managed to keep warm and dry. After all, had we not experienced wet, cold weather in the countries from which we had come? Besides, we were all being subsidized.

Our newfound friends from England, Tony and Brenda, had come laden with a large bag. We were amused. It proved to be a nuisance, interfering with the act of efficient hopping, as they tried to keep an eye on it.

We clapped when the bus, somewhat battered and bruised, finally arrived. Obviously, it had seen better days. Didn't I say that it was subsidized? Never mind! We were out to share an adventure and do a good deed. Did we realize that the bus would be unheated? Not at first. It slowly dawned on us when we were underway. We didn't r-e-a-l-l-y complain. Maybe just a mumble or two to help us keep warm.

Our teeth started to chatter. One antidote was to talk and, then, to keep talking.

We turned to Tony and Brenda, our friends from England. Their teeth were also chattering. They, however, had a different solution. They opened their cavernous bag and withdrew a thermos of steaming hot coffee. Repeated sips did wonders for their shivers and chatters. It did nothing for ours. Not for any one of ours. Not even the aroma.

Dorit's teeth also chattered.

We clapped again, another way to keep warm, when we approached the gate to meet the warden as planned. He had not yet arrived. Since cellphones had not yet been invented, we waited. We waited longer. We could wait no longer. Dorit ventured forward to find either a telephone or a warden, any warden.

She returned. She had called the warden. He had been at home.

"Are you crazy?" He replied. "You can't plant trees in this weather. I'm not leaving the house. Go home!"

"There is nothing for us to do but return. I am sorry." Dorit was apologetic and a little embarrassed.

Nobody complained about turning around and going home. We were all ready.

Tony and Brenda searched their cavernous bag and found another thermos. This time it was steaming hot soup.

How clever of them, we thought. We thought other things as well but they were not nearly as complimentary. The aroma permeated the entire bus. We were unusually quiet.

The next morning found us back in ulpan, warmed, comfortable, and in better spirits,. Ordinarily, we would have been delighted to discuss our adventure and all hands would have flown up at once,. Nobody offered. Not even Dorit. However, it was part of her job. She turned to Vladimir as a way of starting.

"We missed you. You were the only one not to come with us to plant trees."

"I woke up early in the morning," Vladimir answered. "And when I looked out the window and saw that it was raining, I went back to bed."

Dorit stared at him. She was dumbfounded. So were we all. Why hadn't we thought of that? The discussion on planting trees for Tu B'Shvat ended right then and there.

Dorit had other things to discuss . . .

The *Shuk*

"No shuk in America?" Aviva, our Hebrew teacher, was shocked. As immigrants we attended a state subsidized *ulpan* class in order to learn Hebrew and to become acculterated to the state of Israel.

"How do you buy fresh fruit and vegetables? How do you live without a shuk?"

"In America?" We Americans answered, somewhat embarrassed, "In America, we buy everything from the supermarket."

"The supermarket?" Aviva hardly believed the answer. "The supermarket has nothing fresh."

How well we knew that. In great big, rich America we had no choice. In America, the supermarkets bought huge lots of produce, unripe, and stored them until they could put them on the shelves. Frequently, the produce did not mature and turned from unripe green to rot. It was put on the shelves anyway. The customer either bought what was on the shelf or did not buy. There were no other choices.

Here, in tiny Israel, we could go to a shuk, an open market, and check the quality and prices of, sometimes, hundreds of vendors, one next to another, and go to the supermarket as well.

Yet, in the shuk, the rule is "Buyer Beware," for instance, when strawberries are in season. The overwhelming aroma is everywhere and the sight of mounds of deep red fruit as large as unshelled walnuts activate the salivary glands. However much I drool, I must remember to be careful where I buy.

While I am walking around comparing prices and other qualities of the mounds of strawberries, I realize that I am looking at the front of the mound only. The vendor stands on the other side. The mound, should

I have the opportunity to view the vendor's side, may be very different from the front, the customers side. His side may contain yesterday's (or before yesterday's) strawberries which may be half rotten and even moldy. I must remember to buy the strawberries I see and not the ones scooped from the other side. A bargain is not a bargain when half the bargain must be thrown away.

As a rule, I shop in the Jerusalem shuk, Machane Yehuda, weekly. I like to think that I have become wise to its nuances and am a *freier,* sucker, less often. For instance, I look for a stand that has sold most of its berries and only the fresh ones are left. Or I buy the strawberries which are sold in clear plastic boxes and what I see is what I get. Even here, I have to inspect the bottom inside the box. This is done by lifting the box up until it is above eye level until the bottom is visible. It should be dry and without insects. Beware the vendor who will not allow customers to check.

I check also to see if the weight, price per kilo, and the sum total on the scale, are visible. On this point, I have to admit, I have almost given up. So many of the scales are just not visible and I have no way of knowing whether or not the vendor is also weighing a very heavy thumb.

Salmon is the real reason I shop at the shuk. Since we have no meat or chicken in our home, we serve salmon for *Shabbat,* Sabbath, dinner and for evenings when we have company. Like rib steak is to meat eaters, our salmon is to eaters of everything else.

I am being perfectly honest, definitely not bragging, when I say that we have been told repeatedly that we serve the best salmon. It melts in our mouths. I put the salmon in a large dish, skin side down (whether or not it still has its skin. Some fish mongers remove the skin and some do not) and smear it all over with a mixture of lemon juice, fresh minced garlic, Dijon mustard, basil, and one large tablespoonful of mayonnaise. Then it goes into a very hot oven for ten minutes, remains in the oven for another ten minutes with the heat turned off. Then the oven door is left slightly ajar until it's ready to be served. We lick our fingers.

The preparation is only part of the story for the salmon being delectable. The secret is the fish itself. I invariably buy salmon in the shuk from one fish monger, Chaim, and his helper, Yaseem. Yaseem does not ask me what I want. He knows what I want.

He just asks me, "How much? Two kilo? More?"

Then he takes a large, whole salmon from the refrigerator and cuts the head off. Yaseem measures off the amount that I want from that end. That's where the salmon is thickest and has fewest bones. Then he cuts the piece in half and removes the spine and large bones. He does not make a filet. If he made a filet he would remove all of the small bones with tweezers and the fish would cost twenty shekels more per kilo. This way we remove the small bones with our fingers while we eat. Messy, but twenty shekels per kilo is twenty shekels per kilo. And the taste is the same.

At five for three shekels, the biggest bargain in the shuk is freshly baked pita. On a damp, chilly winter day, the smell of warm pita draws us, as the Pied Piper drew children, to a stand where a large wooden tray of pita, hot out of the oven, is laid out evenly in rows. The smell acts as a magnet to draw other shoppers as well. The wooden trays are emptied in minutes. As quickly as the fresh pita is sold, it is replaced.

Sometimes if we're hungry, cold, and/or tired, the pita exists for only a few seconds away from the stand. Sated and warmed, we continue on our way.

But pita is not the entire story. Not at all. Pita is just the means to an end which is falafel. The pita is either cut in half or an opening is cut into one side in order to form a pouch which is filled with the buyer's choice of: Falafel, hot deep-fried balls made of ground chickpeas and spices, humus, tehina, chopped fresh vegetables, fried eggplant, olives, pickled mixed vegetables, sour pickles and/or french fries. Some falafel stands have *schwarma*, fatty meat roasted slowly on an upright spit, which could be added, also.

Our children, arriving by airplane from a far-off land, make falafel their second stop. Their mouths water before they leave our home. No, no, no, my feelings are *not* hurt. After all, they *do* come to us first. We recognize that there are no falafel stands in the large, prosperous country from which they came, not counting the very few stands peopled by misplaced Israelis. And then the pita would not be fresh. They might as well move here where eating well is known to be the soul of civilization.

Recently, the shuk has become gentrified with jewelry and clothing boutiques and cafes. Busloads of tourists crowd the aisles, taking photos every few feet, getting in the way of serious shoppers like us.

There are still plenty of vendors competing with each other's prices and quality. Chaim and his three sons have opened a fish and chips eatery a short distance from his fish shop. The fish could not be fresher.

Nothing ever stays the same, does it?

Potato Chips

Grubby, greedy, and gluttonous little monsters! Before Shabbat services are over they make a beeline for the *kiddush* table, which has the snacks, and align themselves around their favorite goodies. Most head for the potato chips. I have seen them stand over the bowl, plate in one hand and the fingers of the other curled to grab a multitude of chips. With the last notes of *Amen* still lingering in space, chubby little fists like miniature bulldozers, have filled, emptied themselves onto their plates, and returned for more.

By the time I separate myself from my friends and investigate the *kiddush* table only a few chipped chips are left. Every single Sabbath I am left with itty bitty chipped potato chips. I am not above reaching for the dregs but as soon as I do one or another feisty three year old rushes past me for another helping and cleans the bowl of even those.

I am, also, not inclined to wrestle three year olds. Not even for a whole potato chip. At least not while I'm wearing my Sabbath finery. And then there are their parents. If I win, the monsters would be sure to howl and I would have to cope with *them*.

I would like, each Sabbath, to inform each and every one of these runts that, besides the cake and other delicacies on the table, there are plenty of corn thingies and those square little wheat thingies but they don't give me a chance. Their pudgy little hands aim straight for the potato chips and they miss nothing.

When my turn came to sponsor the *kiddush*, I thought, *Aha, this time I will see to it that I have my whole potato chip. I'll buy an extra bag when I do the shopping. So simple and everybody will be happy.*

Usually the sponsor of the kiddush asks one or two of her friends to help set up the table. Before Sabbath I asked both Natalie and Gloria. They were both willing.

During the service, ordinarily after the rabbi's talk, two or three congregants quietly slink out of the sanctuary. That's when the kitchen comes alive with the mad rush to put all of the food on trays or into bowls and carry them off to the room where the repast is held. Everything must be finished and in order before the service is over.

The Shabbat that I sponsored was a little different. After the rabbi's talk, I looked for my friends and they had disappeared from the sanctuary. *Oh well,* I thought, *I'll just get started without them.*

When I went to the kitchen I found everything already in order. The girls had snuck out earlier, thought that they would surprise me, and took care of everything.

The repast progressed normally. So normal, in fact, that I found myself doing battle with the same greedy, grubby group. The potato chip that I had reserved was gone before I could get to it. Not even crumbs this time. I lost again.

"You must have made a mistake when you went shopping." Natalie said. "There was one bag of potato chips too many. We left it behind in the kitchen."

Jerusalem Bus Ride

Twice a week I travel by bus from one end of Jerusalem to the other to go to school to learn Hebrew and to do battle with Ora, our Hebrew teacher. She is determined to teach me to speak Hebrew. I am determined to teach Ora to speak English. I am winning the battle. Ora's English is improving.

On this day, a balmy spring afternoon, a gentleman with a jacket and tie sat opposite me on the bus. *He must be sweltering,* I thought, disinterestedly. I looked around. The bus was quickly filling up. No other male was wearing a jacket and tie. As a matter of fact, I would not have been surprised to learn that half the men on board would have looked blankly at me had I presented them with either jackets or ties.

The gentleman smiled at me. I ignored him. I am a married woman.

He smiled again. *P-u-leeze,* I thought. I straightened my back, smoothed my hair, and stared out the window, peeking at him out of the corner of my eye. He pulled a scrap of paper with an address in Hebrew from his pocket and offered it to me. He smiled broadly, encouragingly, showing all of his gold-capped teeth.

Aha, I thought. *So that's what this is all about. Here is a new immigrant from Russia, the gold-capped teeth give him away, who can speak neither Hebrew nor English and does not know where he is going.*

I accepted the scrap and read the address. The street name was unfamiliar. Ordinarily, I would have shown the paper to the driver but the bus was so crowded that had I made my way over to him, I would have left dozens wounded and bleeding in my wake.

I scratched my head, rumpling my hair. The gentleman saw my perplexity. I shrugged my shoulders. He panicked. He stood up and prepared to leave the bus.

Now, wait a minute, I thought, motioning him to sit down. *Don't panic!*

He sat down again, shoulders leaning forward with his hands upon his knees, hoping for the best.

Good job, old girl, I thought, *really, very good! Now, what do I do? By telling the Russian gentleman to sit down, I am now responsible for his destination and, maybe, even his destiny and I don't have a clue as to where he is going or, even, whether or not he is on the right bus going in the right direction.*

I looked around at our fellow passengers standing in the aisles. One stood out.

Hmm, now here's a real Israeli, a native Hebrew speaker who could slur his words so that only another Israeli could pretend to understand him. Mind readers, these Israelis.

The telltale clue was a huge bag of fresh rolls dangling from one arm. Had he not been on the bus, he would have had a cigarette dangling from his lips, celebrating his success at the shuk, bargaining, actually shouting and cursing, at the top of his lungs. Did it matter that he didn't need ALL of the rolls? Not really. A bargain is a bargain. If his neighbor wouldn't share his bounty, the birds would.

I tapped the Israeli lightly on his arm. He looked at me and I showed him the scrap. He took it, having seen many such scraps before, seasoned Israeli he. He was perplexed.

We're doing well, I thought. *What have I done to this poor Russian gentleman?*

Suddenly, the Israeli's face lit up. *Of course, I should have known! Have I ever met an Israeli who didn't know the answer, right or wrong, to every question? Never.* He was no exception.

"Two stops after I get off," he said. He returned the paper. I returned the scrap to my Russian gentleman.

Now, we're in business. What could be easier than counting two stops after the Israeli gets off?

We were approaching the center of Jerusalem and there was still a considerable distance to go before we arrived at ulpan. I relaxed a little. Three, four stops went by. The Israeli didn't get off. Now, seven and eight and the Israeli was still there. Where, exactly, was he was going to get off? I decided to ask. He told me. I understood. Ora would have smiled triumphantly.

Would you believe that we were both going to get off at the same stop? Now look at who's panicking? I asked myself.

There was some commotion off to the side of me and I turned in its direction. A very pregnant, attractively bewigged young woman with two little children had just been offered a seat and they were now in the process of settling themselves.

"Ima, he pushed me," bawled one cherub. "She pushed me first, Ima," yelled the other.

Ima smoothed her long, brightly flowered skirt and sat up straight, allowing a centimeter or two of lap on each leg. She deftly separated the two and placed a child on each leg.

"Ima, I'm thirsty," cried one darling babe. "And I'm hungry." howled the other.

Unperturbed, Ima dug her arm into the depths of her cavernous bag and brought forth a drink for one and a half sandwich for the other. Settled and content, Ima put her arms around each child and smiled.

Just the person, I thought. I leaned over and asked her if she would please tell the Russian gentleman where to get off. My bus stop was approaching. She nodded. It would be her pleasure.

I motioned to the Russian gentleman. He understood.

I couldn't wait to tell Ora, in Hebrew, of course.

The Storm Eased

The storm eased. Clouds parted and the warm, golden sun shone from a clear blue sky. Rina stood waiting at the bus stop in front of Hadassah Hospital, Jerusalem. She unzipped her jacket just a little and loosened her scarf. She left her hat in place.

Rina's hat was left in place all of the time, indoors and outdoors, to hide her scalp burnt bare by radiology treatments.

One, two minutes with a machine and then, in large clumps, the thick, curly black hair that had adorned her almost from birth, fell out.

One or two years to live they said. Who would know by looking at me that I have a cancer in my brain eating it up?

Radiotherapy was not Rina's idea. She was just following doctors' orders and this was the best that they could offer. They did not talk of a cure.

How come, me? I took good care of myself and I was healthy. Healthy? I could've posed for all of the magazines in the doctors' offices. I ate good. No junk! Only good, healthy food. And not too much either. Until this, I weighed the same that I weighed thirty-five years ago when we got married. Exercise? I exercised every day and walked for an hour every day. I looked gorgeous.

Everybody said to me at each of my birthdays, "You should live to be 120!" And they meant it, too. I thought I would. I really thought I would.

Rina had had no warning. Always a non-stop talker she suddenly found her jaw locked in the middle of a sentence and the words would not come. She would have to start again. It happened again and, then, again.

How come they don't know why? How come all they know is to set my head on fire and make my hair fall out and to torture me until I die?

Walking was no problem, so far. Rina's arms and legs moved freely and she had complete control over them. Nor was her eyesight affected. Her speech was the problem. Lately, she had been confusing times and dates. Or, maybe, it was just fear and depression.

Anyway, that's the way it is, she thought.

The bus pulled up and, as usual, the driver stopped away from the curb.

Every single time! Why doesn't someone tell him that we're sick people who just came from a hospital and that he has to move closer?

Rina said nothing.

With a mutter the crowd, many of them 'walking wounded', clambered aboard. Rina stood closely behind a frail gentleman with a cane should he need support.

See, there's nothing wrong with my body, just my head. Rina smiled. *Mama always said that I made her a hole in the head with my talking. When I wanted something really bad, even as a kid, I wouldn't stop until I got it.*

Mama, who's got the hole in the head, now? You still don't know and I'm not going to tell you. Tomorrow, I'll bring you your favorite little chocolate cakes. Once I brought you a gorgeous bunch of flowers and you weren't happy.

"How come you didn't bring me my chocolate cakes?"

I won't make that mistake again. I'll let you do the talking and you won't even know. You don't see or hear good or walk anymore. But you still know me when I come. Anyway, most of the time you do. Will you know when I don't come anymore?

Mama, I'll always love you.

A path was made for the old man to sit up front right behind the driver. A sign declared the front seats reserved for the infirm and elderly. Rina found a seat in the middle of the bus next to an Ethiopian woman with a small child on her lap. She smiled at each of them. They smiled back. Their eyes shone and their white teeth flashed from smooth ebony faces.

What a sweet, pretty little girl! What will she do when she grows up? What if she grows up to cure cancer? Everybody like me will walk around and look at the world as if we never saw it before. She'll put all of the cancer workers in all of the hospitals all over the world out of business. All of the doctors, nurses, and scientists will be out of jobs. As far as I'm concerned, they can all become hairdressers.

But I know what they'll do. When you come down to it, they're just plain, ordinary human beings out to do their jobs like everybody else. When everybody's around, they'll smile and say, "Isn't it wonderful? No more cancer." But, quietly, when nobody's watching, they'll shake their fingers at this pretty little girl and blame her for everything.

Rina smiled at her again. *She looks so sweet and innocent on her mother's lap. She doesn't know. How could she? I didn't know. Who could know? And where'll I be when she grows up?*

Rina caught a sob midway in her throat and turned it into a little cough.

The bus pulled up to the shuk.

See, something good comes out even of something bad. Tonight, we'll eat good.

Rina descended and immediately turned around to help a pregnant woman, a small child in her arms, struggle with a stroller. She waited until they were organized and then made her way to buy huge, red-ripe strawberries, fresh humus (chickpea spread), and, best of all, pita bread fresh from the oven and warm to her touch. She smiled at each of her favorite shopkeepers. She chose what she wanted and paid whatever they asked. She smiled but had nothing to say, as she usually did, to any of them. Was it her imagination or did they look surprised?

Not everybody has to know my business. Next time, if I can, I'll talk their ears off.

She took a deep breath and said a little prayer. As if on cue, Rina's cellphone rang and she stopped to answer it.

"Ima, I'm pregnant! I just came from the doctor and he said so, definitely. In six months I'll have David in school but Eli will still be in diapers. Ima, I need you."

Rina laughed and, at the same time, tears, uninvited, ran down her cheeks.

"Ruchele, Mazel Tov!" And then quietly to herself, *I need you, too.*

"I'm at the shuk now on my way back from the hospital. I'll stop over on my way home. We'll celebrate with strawberries, fresh pita and good humus. We'll kiss the children and tell them the good news."

"Ma, I love you!"

Ruchele's crying, too.

"Please don't cry, my little Ruchele. This is not a time to cry. Doctors don't know everything. They know that you're going to have a baby but everything else they don't know. They're just doctors."

Rina had spoken easily and without hesitation. She took a deep breath and said another little prayer. *Am I becoming religious?*

On the way to the bus stop, Rina made a small detour to a shop which sold yarn. She chose a soft, pretty green wool and made sure that she had bought enough to knit a sweater, hat, and booties with at least half left over.

Who knows, there could be twins. Or, maybe, just maybe, there'll be another baby after this. Who listens to doctors? They don't know. And how am I supposed to know?

The bright sun warmed Rina until she felt herself glowing. She untied her scarf and unzipped her jacket completely. Maybe, just maybe, the storm was over.

Our Post Office in Jerusalem

The change in our local post office took me by surprise. Gone was the long line behind a red marker on the floor stretching, especially on a Sunday morning, to outside the door and then some. The post office had been closed early on Friday and closed all day for *Shabbat*, Sabbath.

Instead, the line was replaced by neatly placed rows of chairs. A dispenser at the door provided each entrant with a number. A glance at the number in hand and subtracting it from the number on the screen in front of the tellers' windows revealed the number of people seated and waiting.

Organized! Civilized! Wow, what a difference! Were we still in Jerusalem, Israel? What would a little old lady do now?

Time was on a Sunday morning, when the line was as long as ever, a little old lady, cane in hand, would tap, tap, tap her way slowly from the entrance to the post office, passing each person waiting on line, and stopping when she was alongside the first person in line. The soft hum of small talk came to an abrupt end. Silence, thick and heavy, prevailed.

"Ahem, ahem!" The first man standing in line beside her would clear his throat. "*Geveret!* Lady! Everybody must wait his turn on line." He would point to the line "You will have to go outside to the end of the line."

The little old lady turned her head slowly to look directly into the eyes of the speaker.

"*B'-e-met?* R-e-a-l-ly?" Her eyes opened wide in surprise. She did not move.

The speaker said nothing out loud but much under his breath. His face turned red.

When the next teller became free, the little old lady, unhurriedly, tapped her way over to the window. The rest of us waited in silence.

I took a number, found a seat and waited my turn.

A slow but steady gait announced the arrival of a little old lady. Making her way slowly from the entrance, she passed the number dispensing machine without taking a number and stood in the middle of the room.

Aha! My turn! The screen told no lies. I gathered my things which were spread about my seat and made my way to the window. The little old lady was there before me.

Hey now! That sort of thing is past. Definitely, definitely outdated, I thought.

Silently, I approached the window. Really, I did not give the little old lady a little push, exactly. I just asserted myself a little with an elbow in front of the window and gave the teller my number. Undaunted, the little old interloper passed her letters to the teller.

I scowled, for her and all to see. "Sorry, but it's my turn."

"Did you take a number?" The teller asked the little old lady.

"Number? What number? What do you do with a number in the post office? I have letters not numbers."

"You have to take a number from the machine at the door. Everybody has to take a number. Then you sit down and wait your turn. When you see the number on the screen match the number in your hand, you go to the teller who is waiting for you."

The little old lady pushed her letters closer to the teller. "I already waited a long time." She did not budge.

What choice did I have? I thought. *Wrestle her? I knew who would win and I didn't dare to even try. One of the people waiting in the post office would be a newspaper reporter. He would write a story. Maybe, even, take a photograph. His newspaper would put it on the front page:*

"Little Old Lady Wins Wrestling Match with Bully in Post Office."

All of the other newspapers would copy the story. She would be on television. The entire world would be proud of her. A famous chef would name his newest blintz after her. She would be famous.

I would go to jail for the rest of my life. Win or lose, I would lose. I wasn't going to start up with her.

I sighed and stood back. "We're together," I lied. "She comes before me." I waited a half-hour until she was finished.

Modern technology or not, our Jerusalem Post Office was still our Jerusalem Post Office and little old ladies were still little old ladies.

And, unfortunately, those of us who sighed and waited continued to sigh and wait.

The Newspaper Subscription

Deep satisfaction colored Tali's cheeks rosy pink and her eyes shone like blue steel. She leaned all the way back in her brand new executive desk chair.

That's what it's all about. That's class! A chair that supports me even when I lean back all of the way.

She looked up at Ami, shifting from one foot to another.

All of you are what it's about, too. Your job is to support me, just like the chair supports me, no matter what I do.

"Ami?" This was her signal to Ami that she was listening and he could now speak.

"Peggy Cohen is on the phone. She doesn't understand why they are not receiving the newspaper anymore."

"Tell her that they have to pay us what they owe us."

"She says that the paper owes them. She wants to know why we are not following the schedule Michal set up with them."

"What schedule with Michal? There was no schedule with Michal."

Ami rolled his eyes.

Tali continued, "Michal knows that there was no schedule."

Tali sat up straight and looked into Ami's eyes. "I talked with her yesterday." She paused, making sure that Ami understood. "She knows that there was no schedule. Why should there be a schedule? We do not work that way."

Ami took a deep breath and tried one last time. "Peggy Cohen says that the paper charged them for two and a half months after they cancelled their subscription."

"Tell her to pay up."

Tali went back to her brand new executive desk which was littered from end to end. She leaned forward in her new executive chair to review her new executive desktop starting from the sweeping curved end on the left to the sweeping curved end on the right. Her computer screen had its own place on the right end allowing her to do as she wished with the rest of the desk.

Just look! Tali marveled at how the rich walnut veneer emphasized the intricate patterns of its grains. *I must talk to Avram about a glass top to protect it. And he thought that I had nerve demanding a new desk and chair.*

'I have no budget.' He had said. 'The paper is failing. The last Customer Service Manager left a perfectly good desk and chair. Try it.' He had said. 'You'll like it.'

Tali laughed soundlessly. *They wanted someone tough. Someone who would collect any way he could without being bothered by any of it. Well, they got someone tough. I'll talk to Avram about the glass top this afternoon.*

Ami appeared in the doorway.

"Tali, Peggy Cohen wants to speak with you."

Tali sighed. "Transfer her."

Peggy Cohen wasted no time with niceties. "The newspaper charged us for two and one-half months for newspapers after we cancelled our subscription. We had an agreement with the newspaper through Michal, one of your Customer Service people, to restart our subscription according to a schedule. The schedule was made to repay us for you overcharging us. According to schedule, we were not going to be charged again until we had been repaid for what had been taken out of our account."

"Do you have the agreement in writing?"

Peggy felt her checks grow hot. "No, we do not have the agreement in writing. We did everything by telephone."

Tali sat up straight. She was going to end the conversation by having the last word. "Then it's your word against mine. You can do nothing."

"That's not true. We have our bank statement showing what you took from our account over a month after we cancelled the subscription." Peggy Cohen took a deep breath. "Who is your boss? We want to write to him."

Tali almost shouted. "Send Avram anything you want. It will only come back to me."

Avram looked at the letter and copy of the bank statement his secretary, Ruth, gave him.

"Peggy Cohen called while you were out. She said that they want to go over their account with the bookkeeper."

"Did you talk with Tali?"

"Tali received a copy of the same letter you did. She called to say that she is taking care of it."

Avram gave Ruth the papers to be filed. There was nothing more to be said.

So Tali was right. Peggy Cohen put the telephone in its cradle after talking with Ruth. *It didn't matter that I was telling the truth and that she was lying. It would all come back to her. She was in charge.*

Rage bubbled up slowly from within. *Nobody is going to tell me that I'm helpless. She is only the Customer Service Manager, not God.*

"Sue? You want to sue? It will cost you a fortune.' Yael, the Cohens' lawyer, listened, more or less patiently.

"She's going to tell me that I'm helpless?" Peggy was angry. "That she can do what she wants and that there's nobody to stop her? All those people who work for the paper and she has the last word over everybody no matter what she does? Ridiculous!"

"I r-e-a-l-l-y don't want to handle this. There's just not enough money involved."

"Please! We want to go over our account with their bookkeeper. What's so terrible about that?"

"Write a letter to the CEO and send it registered. And, tell him that unless you hear from them, you'll go to court. Then, if you don't hear from them, go to Small Claims Court."

"How much will it cost for you to send the letter? It'll look more important?"

"One thousand shekels. You don't need me. You can do it yourself."

"Suppose I write the letter and you put it on your stationery."

"One thousand shekels."

Peggy reluctantly put the phone down. *I guess that that's that. Money not only talks, it says the whole thing.*

"I just don't understand. What's so terrible about going over our account with their accountant? Somehow, somewhere, I'm missing something. What? What am I missing? It's beginning to drive me crazy."

"Before you write to the CEO, write to the editor-in-chief." Rachel told Peggy during lunch.

Peggy listened carefully to everything Rachel said. Didn't Rachel have an 'in' on the newspaper? She once had an article printed in the magazine section. Also, even more important than that, she was good friends with the movie editor.

Rachel tore off a piece of roll and dipped it into the saucer of olive oil before stuffing it into her mouth. She chewed slowly, closing her eyes, so that she would not be distracted from squishing the oily blob around in her mouth until it dissolved completely. After she swallowed, she greedily tore off a second piece.

Rachel continued. "He's the boss. He can do anything."

Peggy speared a large lettuce leaf, glossy with pinkish-green salad dressing, and stuffed it into her mouth, leaving the stem dangling, dripping salad dressing onto the center of her bright orange blouse. She surreptitiously dipped her napkin into her glass of water and then noticeably dabbed at the spot. The pinkish-green salad dressing spot on the bright orange blouse now included a fuzzy white aura.

Peggy muttered something inaudible with her head down. Then she looked at Rachel doubtfully. "What does the editor-in-chief have to do with finances?"

"Write to him. Just write to him. Send him an email. I have it straight from the movie editor who, you know, is a friend of mine from the old country. That's exactly what he told me."

Peggy was hesitant, unsure of herself, when she called. Since nobody had answered the telephone when she called the editor-in-chief's, office, she had been asked to leave a message. "I sent an email to Guy, the editor-in-chief, two days ago. Did he receive it?"

An hour later, Mira, the editor-in-chief's secretary, returned Peggy's call.

"Guy wants to know what the problem is." She gave Peggy her full attention, her pen poised over a blank piece of notepaper.

Peggy took a deep breath and told her story as she had told it several times before, stopping twice when she felt her voice break.

"Thank you." Peggy finished, grateful to be talking to someone, anyone, who was willing to listen.

Peggy called again the next day. Again, she left a message. Again, Mira returned her call later in the day.

"May I speak to Guy?" Peggy knew the answer even before she asked.

"Guy would like you to send him an email. He said that he will forward it to the right place. He has nothing to do with circulation and/ or finance."

"I sent him an email in the beginning of the week but, never mind, I will be happy to send him another one today."

An hour later, Peggy called again, prepared to leave another message. When someone, not Mira, answered the phone she was impressed. A person, a real person, wow!

"I would like to know whether Guy received the email I just sent him?"

"Mira will be back next week. Call her then."

No wonder she answered the phone right away. She's just a temp. Not a real person. Peggy rephrased her question. Maybe it will make more sense this time.

"How do I know that Guy received my email? I had sent one earlier in the week and, apparently, he did not receive it."

"His secretary will be in next week."

"You mean Guy does not read his emails? Only his secretary does?"

"Guy is not here right now, either. Call back Sunday."

I'm missing something very basic. Something simple. I feel it. But what is it? What am I missing? The same question kept intruding itself in Peggy's mind both while she was awake and in her dreams.

Tali laughed when she read the email. She still doesn't get it! I told her that it all comes back to me and she didn't believe me. Who else would Guy send this to?

31

Tali picked up her phone and leaned all the way back in her chair. Having a brother-in-law for CEO certainly does not hurt. No, not at all.

"Eitan, you're going to be next. This idiot sent faxes and emails to everyone on the paper. I'm letting you know. I wouldn't even be surprised if she paid her lawyer a fortune to send you a letter. I'm going to send the collection agency after her. That'll really give her something to complain about." Tali giggled. She dabbed at a spot on her smooth, glass-topped desk.

Nice! She thought. *Very, very nice.*

The CEO is next. Peggy's fury lay hidden beneath the surface. *I don't believe that Guy Steins sent the email I sent him to Tali. It was not his department, he told Mira.*

Peggy sat at the kitchen table chopping carrots and tried not to chop her fingers. She was angry and had to be extra careful.

I've done some really stupid things when I've been angry.

Peggy reviewed the newspaper staff. *I started with the Customer Service people. Then their manager. Then her boss. The editor-in-chief was, so far, the last. All that's left is to find out that the CEO is a close relative of hers.*

Sending a letter to the CEO will take a letter from our lawyer. I'll call her again. And then, again, if I have to.

Peggy stopped chopping carrots, narrowly missing her thumb, and sat up straight. Laying the chopping knife aside, she walked over to the phone and dialed her lawyer.

"You do not need me." Yael answered. "Write a letter to the CEO and send it registered. Say that if you do not hear from him, you will go to court. Do not say the Small Claims Court. Just court. Say that you are taking the newspaper to court. That should be enough."

"Did Eitan receive my registered letter? I sent it last week and I have not yet heard from him." Peggy had difficulty sounding confident.

"I'll find out and call you back." Eitan's secretary spoke lightheartedly.

She did not call back and Peggy was not surprised. Peggy did not bother to call again.

Yet I'm missing something. Something important. Something basic. The feeling nagged at her.

Peggy sat up straight. Of course. That's the answer. It's simple. It's basic. Why didn't I think of it before?

"I want to talk to the manager of the accounting department, please." *My last resort at the newspaper. That's what I've been asking for all along, an accountant to go over our account line by line. I should have gone directly to the accounting office. No wonder I'd felt that I was missing something important. It should have been the first thing to do after I spoke with Tali.*

"I have been a subscriber for fifteen years and I want to go over the last year of my account."

"I'll transfer you to someone who could help you."

"Thank you." Peggy waited, holding her breath. *Really! So simple! No wonder something was bothering me. Why not just go to the accounting office on my own?"*

"Customer Service," someone replied brightly.

Peggy hung up. *So much for my nagging instinct. So much for the feeling that I was missing something important and simple. It just didn't know what it was talking about.*

She sat in place for a few minutes without moving, as if she were a balloon, deflated, diminished and empty.

Well, that's that. It all goes back to Tali. Unbelievable!

*I just don't understand. She could be overcharging, undercharging as she pleases and there is **no one** checking up on her? Isn't the newspaper a business? How is it still in business?*

There is no alternative but to go to the Small Claims Court.

Peggy filed her complaint in triplicate. Peggy was nearly shaking. *I'll have to control my voice.*

"What is your complaint?" The judge asked.

"We cancelled the newspaper subscription that we had had for fifteen years on the first of December, 2008. In January 2009 the *horat kevah*, standing order, on our bank was charged 615NIS. We cancelled our 'standing order' with the bank but the money had already been paid to the newspaper. We called Customer Service and spoke with Michal. After several conversations, we agreed to renew our subscription with the money being paid back to us according to a schedule. We would receive the newspaper without payment until we had been repaid."

"What schedule?" Tali's voice was shrill. "There was no schedule. You have nothing in writing."

"We have a letter from you. Four letters actually, all saying the same thing. You sent us a letter in Hebrew and one in English by email. You sent us the same letter in Hebrew and a separate one in English by postal delivery. Not one of them makes any sense." Peggy pulled Tali's letters from her folder. "Not one of them mentions the money you took from us after we cancelled the subscription. We have the bank statement. Not one of them mentions that we suspended delivery for five weeks while we were outside the country over Passover." Peggy removed the boarding passes from her folder.

"What about your credit card?" Tali rose to her full height. Now, the judge would understand. "We couldn't charge your credit card. Your credit card company refused to pay us." Now her voice was shrill. "We don't give newspapers away for free!"

Peggy also stood tall. She looked directly at Tali. "You didn't charge our credit card! You kept charging our 'standing order' which we had cancelled after you took more than six hundred shekels from it in January. We gave Michal our credit card number which was to have been used to pay for the newspapers which would have been delivered to us after we had been repaid for the money you took from us. You were not supposed to charge our credit card until you repaid the money you took from us in January." Peggy was angry. "Do you know what you're doing? Do you really understand what you're doing?"

Tali turned to the judge. "Who does she think she is? She wants free newspapers. Nobody gets free newspapers."

Peggy kept going. "You owe us over three hundred shekels. The newspapers we received until you cut off delivery were worth about three hundred shekels. You still owe us over three hundred shekels from the over six hundred you took from us in January after we cancelled the newspaper subscription. Pay us what you owe us!"

"You owe US three hundred shekels!" Tali waved a copy of one of the letters that she had written, "You pay us!"

Peggy turned to the judge again. "We want more than three hundred shekels. We miss the newspaper for breakfast. For fifteen years we read the newspaper while we had a cup of coffee. Now, we want two computers for six thousand shekels so that we could both read the newspaper online while we have breakfast. If we can't have the newspaper in our hands at least we will have the newspaper another way."

For a moment, the judge said nothing. Then, surprising himself, he laughed. He stopped for a moment to reconsider his reaction and, then, he roared with laughter. Two computers at the breakfast table? What an idea! Why not? Why didn't I think of that myself?

Tali stood with her mouth open. She was stunned.

The judge turned to Tali. "Do you still say that you did not charge their 'standing order' after the subscription was cancelled? Do you still say that you delivered newspapers after these people had suspended delivery and were in another country? What do you have showing that you charged their credit card and not their 'standing order'?"

Tali's face turned bright red. Hatred shone in her eyes. "You believe her? You don't believe me? Who is she? What is she? She's a nothing. I'm a sabra. My great-great-grandfather built Petach Tikvah. My grandfather fought in the Palmach with Ben Gurion. SHE came here fifteen years ago and right away she wants a newspaper with her coffee. And for FREE! She wants it for free!"

Tali dared the judge to make a decision.

He looked directly at Tali. "Unless you demonstrate that what you say in your letter is correct, I will find in favor of the Cohens. You will have to pay them compensation, six thousand shekels, which is the price for two computers."

The Cohens hugged each other. They would have hugged the judge as well had they been permitted.

"I'm a reporter for the other newspaper." A young man gave the Cohens his calling card as they were leaving the courtroom. "I came to sit in on a case which is up after yours." He showed his camera. "Do you mind if I take a photo of you?"

Peggy and Ezra posed.

"I'd like to have more details. Do you mind if I ask you a few questions?"

The article and photo appeared the following morning. That same afternoon, the Cohens received requests to be interviewed by radio and television stations. They told their story simply but, invariably, the interviewer had to laugh. Why not side-by-side computers while having a second cup of coffee?

The month after the newspaper lost the lawsuit, the list of staff member printed on the inside page had changed. Tali was no longer listed as a staff member.

Challenge

Every morning I wake to the challenge of coping with the sour, empty feeling in my gut that war is imminent. Every morning in Jerusalem, during the month of February, in the year 2003, I am oppressed by the possibilities of being bombed by crazed murderers or hit by missiles loaded with explosives, germs, and/or chemicals. Is there a greater threat than the threat to the existence and way of life of myself and of all whom I love? In a moment, all could be gone as if it had never been.

On this gray morning, birds are visiting me on my balcony. Perching on the rail the cheery little things bob up and down and then hippity-hop across the stone before they fly off. I sincerely hope that on this day they find juicy worms and tasty insects and grow and prosper and feed their young. Do they know, do they not know, that disaster looms? Are they better off not knowing?

Selfishly, I shoo them off.

Please birds, find uncultivated fields to have your meals and to leave your telltale calling cards. Should a balcony such as this one be more convenient for you, I could point the way, even give you a road map, to my landlord's balcony.

They may not know whether or not their lives will be brought to a cruel, abrupt end. But, then again, neither do I.

On the way to the bus stop, I pass a flower stand. The daffodils catch my eye. As bright a yellow as the morning sun, their fluted trumpets announce the coming of spring. I buy a bunch because . . . , well, just because. Just because life is beautiful and I no longer take it for granted.

The bus is crowded but I find a seat.

Across from me, a cranky child tries to find a comfortable place on his mother's lap. I give him a flower. He stops his squirming, smiles, and shows his mother. She smiles in return.

The Arab gentleman with gnarled, arthritic fingers sitting next to me removes a bunch of rosemary from his bag and gives me a sprig. I put it to my nose, inhale its fragrance, and smile in gratitude. He passes branches out to others who also put them to their noses and smile.

Nobody says a word. We may not speak the same language. No matter, we understand. All of us want to live, love, and be loved. Today, I am especially aware.

In the center of the city, I get off the bus to meet my friend, Carol, at the Rimon Cafe for a cup of coffee and a little conversation. Well, a cup of coffee, certainly, a little snack, perhaps a chocolate croissant, and a LOT of conversation. Retirement earns us these simple pleasures.

On the way to our meeting, I think about the instructions that I received in the mail in Hebrew and in English on how to prepare for a missile attack. I have the gas mask issued some years ago and recently updated. Now I have to make a room airtight and equip it with water, food, and necessities to make it safe and comfortable. I make a mental list.

A long scarf, iridescent with bright and lively colors, hanging on a hanger outside a shop captures my attention. I buy it and wrap it around my neck with long tails left flapping. Who knows, it may be needed as a tourniquet. I am enrolled in a first aid class.

Carol is seated and waiting for me. Her husband is not well. Their son is closing his shop and their grandchildren are very upset. The times are not good and the economy is suffering. We have coffee and croissants and I commiserate.

I invite Carol to walk with me to the shuk to buy fresh strawberries. The shuk has the best strawberries: Plump, dark red, and fragrant. I drool. Carol has other plans. I give her the rest of the flowers. They cheer her.

The sky darkens and rain is in the air. I am definitely not complaining. Nobody in water-poor Israel complains about the rain:

"Isn't the rain wonderful?" We all say as we look for extra sweaters.

"I'm so excited! Have you heard that the Kinneret, the Sea of Galilee, is rising and that there are four feet of snow on Mount Hermon?" We bake cookies to warm ourselves.

"As soon as the roads will open, we will ride up to the Golan and take the ski lift to the top of Mt. Hermon. We'll throw snowballs at each other and take lots of photos." There is a mad hunt for our boots and gloves. As soon as our noses run and our throats become sore, the hunt includes scarves and warm hats, as well.

"We've prayed for rain and, look, our prayers are being answered." We decide not to go outside but to leave the fun and excitement to the next generation.

We have something hot to drink, and go to bed.

I walk quickly along Jaffa Road bypassing shops on the way. The aroma of freshly baked pita, bread, and cake warm me and I know that I am close to the shuk.

A young man, bowed with the weight of a heavy backpack, gets out of the back seat of a car, crosses the street, and walks alongside me. The wide, fixed smile on his face catches my attention. He does not look at me or at anybody else but walks steadily and purposefully. His expression does not change. Is the aroma of freshly baked bread and ripe strawberries enticing him as it does me?

Somehow, I do not think so. I see a wire leading from his pocket to his backpack. The sight of the wire shocks me. With all my might, I push him into the street and I grab his hands. A car screeches and almost hits us.

"Terrorist! Terrorist!" I scream.

The driver leaves his car and together we pin him down. Others come. The police are called. Two policemen and a police car arrive at the same time. His hands are handcuffed behind his back and more police arrive.

Still shaking, I realize that it is raining and that I am being pelted. Huge raindrops are attacking my eyeglasses so that it is hard for me to see. I buy strawberries and warm pita bread and decide to go home.

All of life is a challenge. I come to the conclusion as I board the bus. This is who I am, where I live, what the times are and I'm doing my best.

I look around the bus at my fellow travelers and relax. I smile. I'm in good company.

The Jerusalem Volunteer Police Force

"Are you real policemen or are you dressed in Purim costumes?"

Charlie and I looked at each other and we burst out laughing. Charlie stretched himself tall and towered over little Queen Esther in her gown and crown. An old-school male chauvinist, he answered for both of us.

"We are real policemen and we are wearing real uniforms."

The question would have been reasonable even if it were not Purim. Little Queen Esther was older than Charlie's great-granddaughter and younger than my granddaughter.

Our duties, as volunteer policemen for the city of Jerusalem, were to establish a presence in public places especially in those areas frequented by tourists. We were required to speak both English and Hebrew. A couple of us also spoke Arabic. We were to uphold the law and to be alert to any possible public danger. We carried guns for which we were trained to maintain and use. We were to coordinate with the regular police force and augment it.

"Take pity on your children!" I once yelled at a man with two young sons crossing the street against the light. He stopped short, realized what he was about to do, and retreated. His "Thank you!" made my day.

Here, in Jerusalem, we did not expect to be thanked. For instance, there was this old lady with a cane about to cross a busy intersection on Keren Hayesod Street without paying any attention to the lights or traffic. Whether she was intent on killing herself or not was not our business. Our job to make sure that she did not. We stopped her and, very solicitously, reminded her to watch out for traffic lights and to cross only at crosswalks. She ignored us. We stood over her and glowered.

What she screamed at us was earthy, colorful, and unrepeatable. We stood our ground. She gave in and waited for the light to change.

Did we expect gratitude for saving her life? We were happy to see her reach the other side safe and sound. Our patrol continued.

Our volunteer police unit was divided up into patrols which toured different parts of the city. For instance, one patrol covered the parks and hotel areas, another, a popular tourist spot which was a major lookout point over the city with trails and picnic areas, and another, the shopping areas. Our patrol (usually Charlie, Joe, Jon, and I) was assigned to cover the city center shopping areas.

The day Charlie and I encountered little Queen Esther, Joe was not with us. Had he been, he would have answered instead of Charlie. Not only did Joe outrank Charlie but he was a retired school principal and teacher who never stopped teaching. Queen Esther would have learned about the importance of good citizenship until her eyes crossed.

Joe's pet peeve was illegally parked cars. "Move your car immediately," he would order the driver of a car parked in a no-parking area. He would also point out those areas where it was permissible to park.

Most of the time, Joe had his wish and the driver moved his car without comment. Other times, he would receive an argument. "I'm here only for a moment." Or, "As soon as I deliver something or receive something or somebody comes or until I finish eating." In essence, Joe would be ignored.

Then he would swing into action. With a flourish, he would take out his notebook and pen and, making sure that the driver was watching, copy the license plate number. That was usually enough to make the driver move.

But, even then, sometimes, the driver refused to budge. Joe would then snap his notebook shut, put his pen away, and we would be on our way. Joe, like other volunteer policemen, lacked the authority to issue parking tickets.

Jon was pleasant, well-meaning, and deaf despite two hearing aids. He tried to hide his deafness with a booming voice that hardly stopped to take a breath. How else could he be part of the conversation?

Should a tourist happen by with a question, for instance, about directions or need simple advice, Jon would take a deep breath and lecture at length on the beauty and wonders of Jerusalem and Israel. If the tourist did not excuse himself and go elsewhere, Jon would end with a passionate declaration of love for his country and his people.

Around the corner and out of sight, the tourist could always find another tourist willing to help him.

Besides providing a presence on the street and being helpful, we always kept our eyes open for anything unusual.

For instance, during the middle of one hot and dusty summer day's patrol on Ben Yehuda Street, when we were looking forward to our coffee break, I noticed a large bag propped up against a seat outside a café. *What a nice looking diaper bag*, I thought absentmindedly, absorbed in my eternal, internal struggle about whether to have a croissant with my coffee or not. I had been fighting a losing battle with the bathroom scale.

I stopped short. "Diaper bag?" I said aloud. "Where's the baby?" The area was deserted. We made a wide circle around the bag and waited.

Little Mother, I thought, *Please come and pick up your baby's diaper bag so I could have my hard-earned coffee and chocolate croissant.*" I had decided on chocolate.

We waited a few minutes and then, reluctantly, gave up. Charlie called the bomb squad to come and detonate the package. In the meantime, we had to clear the area. We asked everybody in the shops to please keep away from glass windows. Of course, they all rushed to the front to see what was happening.

In the rest of the world, everybody runs away at the first sign of danger. In Jerusalem, everybody has to know, and, of course, give advice. The bomb squad arrived. The bag was blown up. There had not been a bomb inside. We relaxed.

One minute after the bag was destroyed, however, a young woman, half-running, half-walking, pushing a baby carriage as fast as she could, stopped at the spot where the bag had been.

"That was my diaper bag from Land's End. I have a cheap plastic bag at home. *That*, you could have blown up!"

Haven't I already said something about not expecting gratitude? We had not even had our coffee. Coffee break time was over and I would have to have my chocolate croissant another time.

Shahid

I am going to Paradise. I will sit at the feet of Allah and serve him forever. We will praise and honor each other for all eternity. There will be open fields and the sun will shine on us all of the time. We will shower each other with flowers of all shades and hues and they will live forever and disappear only when a gentle breeze will whisk them away.

My father will be proud of me and my mother will weep for joy. My brothers and sisters will talk of me in awed and hushed whispers with a deep longing and envy for the honor that only I, a *shahid*, a martyr, can bring the family.

Tonight I will leave the house when nobody will know and meet Achmed and his friends who will have the belts for us. Then they will make a video of us holding the Koran and telling everyone we love that we are going to go to serve Allah with joy in our hearts. The blood of the Jews will be the carpet on which we walk to Paradise and their cries of agony the music that will wave us on and speed us on our way. Palestine first and then, with the will of Allah, the world will be Muslim and it will be because of us.

I am telling you this because I want you to know how I feel. I want you to know how it is that an ordinary girl like me with eight brothers and sisters and not yet married came to be chosen.

I was surfing the internet after everyone had gone to bed and I saw the message: "Only those who love Allah and want to serve him should contact me." It was signed, "Achmed."

Of course, I love and want to serve Allah. Even as a small child, I thought only of Allah and his glory. I always did as I was told and I knew that Allah would be pleased. So, I answered Achmed and told him how

I felt. And he answered me. Then we had a meeting. There were others like myself.

Achmed, strong and handsome, told us that it was Allah's will that Palestine be ours and that the world be Muslim. That only we who serve Allah with all of our hearts and souls could do Allah's work. He told us that we are special and that we are pure and that all of our earthly sins count as nothing when we do Allah's work.

Then he said that if anyone wants to leave, he should leave. The door was not locked and that nobody would be stopped from leaving. "There is no shame in leaving," he said. "Go! Leave!" He said.

I looked at Achmed and looked at the door and then I looked at my feet so that nobody could see the shame in my eyes. Who would be the first to leave? There was only silence. Nobody left.

I tell you the truth. I was scared but what else could I do? Could I have been the first one to get up and leave? Could I have said that my fear was stronger than my will to serve Allah? No, I could not! Allah conquers all!

The meeting was over. While walking home, I took a deep breath. The air smelled heavy and sweet like the perfume of roses. The ground was soft and I felt that I was walking on a rich and heavy carpet. A breeze caressed me all the way home.

So, my friend, I go with my head held high. Remember me well! Cry with joy when you see my picture. All of my unborn children will surround me in Paradise. My husband-to-be, whom I have never met and, perhaps, strong and handsome like Achmed, will also cry when he sees my picture. My husband, my lover, will be Allah.

So, my friend, you will keep my secrets within your heart and tell no one. I cannot be stopped now. Paradise awaits me. I have enough of earthly pleasures. You will tell no one. Not my father, not my mother, not any one of my brothers or sisters. You will not go to school and whisper quietly what you have heard me say. Not to my classmates and not to our teacher. Nobody could stop me from following Achmed and doing Allah's will. Nobody!

The Reporter

Mahmoud looked away as his editor spoke to him.

"Cover the demonstration against the wall the Jews are building to keep us out and report on their Israeli army Nazi brutality. Take your cousin, J'bril with you. He's a good photographer. Take a couple of boys, too. Omar collected a big pile of stones this morning and put them by a bush. You'll know where to look."

It's a job. Just a job, Mahmoud thought, *but he knows that I'm good at it. That's the problem.*

Mahmoud signaled J'bril and the two trudged to a car marked "Press". They had been to demonstrations before. On the way they stopped outside a school where children were standing around.

"You! And you!" Mahmoud beckoned to two boys to come over. *Not too old. Not too little.*

"Want to make fifty shekels apiece?"

The boys' faces lit up.

"Come with us. You will find a pile of stones waiting for you." Mahmoud winked at the boys. "You know what to do with them.

There was a time, Mahmoud thought, *when it was better. There was a time when Jews came to our villages to shop and we welcomed them. There was a time when my cousins in Ramlallah came here to visit us and we went there to visit them whenever we wanted.*

That was before Arafat. I never wanted Arafat. Nobody did. Why did the Jews bring him and his gangsters here from Tunis? What did the Jews need him for? Life was better before he came.

"Over there. There." Mahmoud had been through all this before. "You see where our people are shouting at the soldiers. You see where the soldiers make a human chain to push them back. Stand behind the shouters and throw rocks at the soldiers. Hit them in their heads. Aim for their eyes. When you are finished, crouch down low and run away."

The boys ran eagerly to their positions.

"Ho, *chaver,* buddy! Mahmoud!"

Mahmoud turned to recognize Daniel from the previous demonstration. *We covered the same event but who would believe it? Not anyone reading each of our newspapers. Different bosses. Different angles. The Jews read their newspapers and we read ours. So far, I haven't heard any complaints. We'll probably see each other again at the next demonstration.*

"Daniel! We meet again. Are you having a good time? All you Jews want is a good time."

"And all you Muslims ever want is trouble. I tell you, you do a good job. Wherever you are there's trouble."

They both laughed.

"Why don't you give me a call sometime and we'll sit down together for a coffee or, maybe," Daniel winked at Mahmoud, "A beer."

Daniel fished around in his pocket for his calling card.

"No need to bother. You gave me your card last time. I still have it." Mahmoud shrugged. "See you at the next demonstration."

J'bril positioned himself so that he could take photos of the demonstrators screaming and shouting, their voices shrill with derision and hatred, being pushed back by the chain of soldiers.

When the army used tear gas the crowd dispersed.

A few of the demonstrators, eager to have their stories in the morning newspaper, ran over to Mahmoud who was clearly marked "Press." They were still shouting.

"They were shooting bullets. If the pigs could aim better, we'd be dead."

"They killed our fathers and our sons. Now they want to kill us, too."

"We want our land back. My family was here for thousands of years and they stole our land from us."

Mahmoud had heard it all before but still recorded every word. *They're well-rehearsed,* he thought. *I'll just add a little more color and make it just a little juicier. The more I write about Israeli brutality, oppression and aggression, the better it'll sell. The truth?* He sneered. *That's supposed to be what I'm here for, isn't it?*

Nobody has to know about the rocks. Mahmoud looked at J'bril who was putting his equipment away. *Who would believe that one of the soldiers was lying on the ground with blood running down his face? J'bril saw him also. Let the Israeli photographers take those pictures.*

Coffee cup on the table, Mahmoud opened the paper the next morning to see his article and J'bril's photos cover the top half of the front page. He sat up straight. *This could make the media the world over. This is _real_ money!* He could almost feel it. *I made it big time.* Automatically, he put his free hand in his pocket to jiggle coins while smiling with deep satisfaction.

Then, he leaned back in his chair and took a deep breath. *This is what I have been waiting for, dreaming about. Now I have something to show my future father-in-law.*

The house was on top of the hill and the drive up to it was pleasant. As the car climbed the houses became increasingly larger and more elegant. Mahmoud found the right address and parked.

He walked slowly towards the front door. *I own my own car and my own home. I have an education. I have a job. I am a young man and I can give my bride everything.*

He thought of Mona, his cousin J'bril's cousin. He had been introduced to her at a family wedding. She had looked boldly into his eyes at first and then, smiling shyly, looked away. Her eyes had shone like ripe, black olives and her skin was smooth and clear. Mona had blushed. Mahmoud grew excited when he thought of her.

Mahmoud hesitated just a moment. *I'm wearing a western style suit and tie. I brought my last bank statement and a few of the articles I wrote including the last one. What else could I have done?* Then he knocked on the door.

Maher, Mona's father, welcomed Mahmoud into his home according to custom as if he were an old friend and they had done this many times before. Each knew what the visit was about and there was no need to rush. The pastries, fruit and coffee had each to be tasted and small talk had to be made.

Mahmoud sampled each delicacy set before him, commenting on the pleasure it had given him while sipping coffee between each bite. He allowed Maher to lead the small talk on the weather and the world situation and waited patiently for the right moment.

When the right moment presented itself, Mahmoud sat up straight and looked directly into Maher's eyes.

"I want your daughter, Mona, for my wife. I will be good to her." Mahmoud reached for his briefcase, fumbling with its latch. *Where did I put my bank statement?*

Maher's smile left his face. "And what is it that you do for a living?"

"I am a reporter. A very good one. I will give you a copy of the last report I wrote. It will be published in newspapers all over the world."

"Yes, I understand. You make a lot of money. But it is a dangerous job. Is it not? Sometime, like others before you, you will write something that will make a politician or gang leader angry and he will have to teach you a lesson. If you will be lucky, you will be taken to jail and beaten. If you are not so lucky, you will be shot in your knees so that walking will be difficult for you for the rest of your life. If you make another mistake and be even less lucky, you will be found in a ditch somewhere with your face down in the water.

"I want my daughter to have a good life with her husband and children. How could I want otherwise? With you, she will become a widow too soon. I cannot say 'yes.' I am sorry."

Mahmoud, by this time, had found all of the papers he had brought and had put them in order. By the time Maher had finished speaking, the papers hung loosely in Mahmoud's hand. He had wanted to argue but could not. Maher was right. The last reporter murdered had been a friend. They had both written for the same newspaper. From time to time they had worked together.

After the murder the reporters gathered together and demonstrated. Mahmoud stood with them. They stood and shouted for a long time. Afterwards each one went home.

Disappointed, Mahmoud left the house and walked towards his car. On the way he turned his head to look back. Mona was watching him from her window. He raised his hand to smooth his hair but halfway up his head, waved to her, just slightly, in case anyone was watching. She waved back.

Mahmoud tried to forget Mona. *There is more in life than marriage,* he told himself. But the more he tried, the more she appeared to him in his thoughts and in his dreams. Once he thought he saw her walking down the street. He ran after her and then found that it was someone else.

Mahmoud leaned over the table in the coffee house to look directly at J'bril.

"I called you to meet me here because I didn't know what else to do. I am going crazy. Mona is in my head. I see her eyes wherever I go and when I dream, I dream only of her. I must see her. I must talk with her. Nothing else in my life is important. Tell me what to do!"

J'bril smiled. "I saw Mona at another wedding and we had a little talk. She feels as you do. Everything you said I have heard from Mona. I swear by Allah it is so. She also wants me to help her. Leave it to me."

They met in the back room of the dress shop. J'bril had made the arrangements. Mahmoud would enter through a back door and Mona would enter the shop from the front. The back room was never visited by anyone else while they were there. They were not the first lovers to find a safe haven in the shop.

Shy at first, they sat apart and spoke about their families and then about themselves. Each time they met they moved closer to each other than they had been before until they intertwined and became lovers. They thought of little else but of their last meeting and counted moments until they met again. The door would hardly close before they would rush into each other's arms.

Mahmoud entered the room behind the dress shop smiling, one day, only to have the smile disappear as he looked at Mona. She had been waiting for him. She had been crying. More tears made rivers down her face as she spoke.

"My father wants me to marry Saeb. "I told Baba that I do not want to marry. Not Saeb. If I cannot marry you, I will marry no one. No one. He said that he had already told Saeb that it was alright."

Mona stood up and paced. "Saeb is a law professor at Bir Zeit University. Baba says that he is safe. He says that he even teaches to policemen. Who would kill him the way they would kill a reporter?"

Mona's voice was shrill. "I have to have a way out. I will be a *shahid*. Better a martyr than a life without you." The tears flowed freely.

"*Shahid?*" Mahmoud, horrified, grasped Mona by her shoulders and held her tightly. "We will find a way. I promise you that we will find a way."

Mahmoud left the dress shop and called J'bril. He had already planned to call him because another demonstration was going to take place the next day and he did not want to go. Now he needed his cousin and best friend to help him think.

J'bril was more than eager to meet. He was agitated and his voice was shrill. "The café. Yes. Yes. The café. Five minutes. Ten minutes. I will be there."

J'bril picked his coffee cup up and put it down again. He took a sip of water. Then he put the coffee cup to his lips but did not drink.

"They want me to help them. Help them? I think that they are crazy! Why are they doing this? For money? Just for money? They want to blow up the tallest building in Tel Aviv. They want to bring Al Qaeda here like they brought it to America. Are they not crazy? What will happen to me if I help them? What will happen to me if I don't?"

J'bril looked first to his right and then to his left. Was anyone listening, anyone watching? He had chosen a table in a far corner so they would be alone.

"They are going to use three trucks. The trucks and the explosives are already hidden in different places in Israel. If they surround the building with three trucks and then explode them at the same time, they will bring the building down. It is Saeb's idea. All of the men are policemen from his class. They have been working on this for a long time."

J'bril brought the cup to his lips once more. "They want me to take photographs of everything from the time they put the trucks in place to the explosion and after the explosion. They want the world to know what happened right under the noses of the Israelis.

"They will be killed. I will be killed." J'bril hissed between his teeth. "I am not ready to die!"

Mahmoud sat expressionless. The stillness masked the horror that paralyzed him. He had not said a word since they met. His eyes betrayed him. They never left J'bril's face.

Mahmoud spoke calmly. "Give me time. I will think of something. I promise you."

Didn't I just say that to Mona? He thought. *Promises! How many promises am I making? What a liar I've become. How can I make promises when I don't know what to do?*

"I came to talk to you about the demonstration tomorrow." Mahmoud said absentmindedly. He was trying to think. He felt that he had to say something.

"Demonstration tomorrow?" Mahmoud repeated, stopping short with a sudden shock as he heard his own words. He suddenly sat up straight, opening his eyes wide.

After a moment's pause, Mahmoud leaned across the table and spoke slowly and softly but very clearly to J'bril.

"I have an idea but, first, you must do something for me. You must tell Mona that I have to see her tomorrow at the shop. Tell her that she must be there as soon as it opens. She must tell her father that she has thought about the wedding and is going to look for a wedding dress. Then she will tell her father that she will stay with your mother for a few days to think about the wedding and to be alone. Tell your mother that she is to say that Mona is with her."

That night, Daniel, sleepy from a full day's work, downloaded his emails, as was his habit, before he went to bed. Eyelids ready to close, he opened one after the other. "Ha, ha!" Delete. "*Tsk, tsk!*" Delete. Then he stopped short. *What's this?* Suddenly wide awake, Daniel read the message again. And, then, once more, to be sure.

"You are coming with us to the demonstration, today." Mahmoud did not explain to Mona when they met at the shop. The less she knew, the better, in case something went wrong.

Mona did not care. Red-eyed from a sleepless night on a pillow soaked with tears, she was ready to do anything Mahmoud asked.

"I don't want you to go home. You will wait here for an hour and then go to the market near the news agency. As soon as you see us leave to go to the car, go to the back seat and bend down. There will be a package of my little brother's clothing on the floor. Put it on."

Mona did as she was told. The news assignment was identical to the one before. His boss' voice droned on in bored disdain: J'bril, the stones, and the boys. *Good,* Mahmoud thought. *I don't need any surprises.*

As soon as Mahmoud and J'bril left the office, Mona joined them in the car. She lay as low on the floor as she could until she had changed clothes and then she sat up.

This time they did not pick up any boys.

"There they are! Those are the troublemakers! And a stone throwing little murderer with them!" The red-faced Israeli army commander roared at them at the top of his lungs. Everyone turned around to listen. He had been waiting for them at the entrance to the parking lot.

"I read your article! I saw your photos! So did everyone else in the world. Who the hell do you think you are? We don't shoot until you shoot first. You kill our wives and children in cold blood and you scream brutality. And your land?" The commander became derisive. "Your land? Most of you came after we Jews. Most of you came for jobs as we settled the country. The world doesn't need your lies!"

"The demonstration is off limits to all of you! Don't even think of getting out of your car! Roll up your windows and stay inside. You see that car pulling up in front of you? Follow it! We don't need trouble making garbage like you anywhere near here!"

Nobody in the automobile said a word until they arrived at military headquarters.

They were interviewed separately. J'bril was called in first. He told the commanding officer everything he knew including names and dates. Mahmoud was next and then Mona had her turn.

Daniel arrived soon after, grinning broadly. "Great demo! You guys missed the best one yet. Some of your friends found a pile of rocks under a bush and went to town. The lousy bastards hit a couple of our guys and then the tear gas. You should have heard the screams:

"The Israel murderers used real bullets. They can't aim. Real bullets!

"An ambulance! Get an ambulance! Three people are on the ground. They can't get up."

And then they smashed the cars and trucks. They didn't care whether they were Jewish or Muslim. They just went wild." Daniel laughed. "Then they didn't know how to get back home. Bedlam! Pure bedlam! What they missed was a good photographer like you, J'bril. Nobody is going to publish the story without good photos. You're just what my newspaper needs. How about if I bring all of you back to the office to meet the boss?

"After that, lunch on me." Daniel felt expansive, even generous. "I know a great pizzeria."

J'bril and Mahmoud were hired by Daniel's newspaper. J'bril's skill as a photographer and Mahmoud's reputation as a reporter were widely known. Daniel's boss felt fortunate to be able to make them team members.

After lunch, Mahmoud, Mona, and J'bril visited their relatives in Jerusalem who found places for them to stay.

The next morning Israel Radio announced that the army had arrested an university professor and three policemen planning to carry out a major attack in Tel Aviv.

With the help of their relatives, Mahmoud and Mona were married in Jerusalem. Mahmoud wrote a book about his experiences allowing the public an uncensored view of the world from which he had come. His book was well received. Both Mona and he were content with their lives until J'bril was murdered. He was found face down in a ditch. His body showed signs of torture.

The army found the murderers in Ramallah. They confessed and revealed who had commissioned them. The murder of J'bril was to have set an example for others.

Soon after, Mahmoud was offered and accepted a teaching position in an American university. Mona and he settled there and raised their family in comfort and security in a new land.

Love Story

Eight months old and without a cover! What else could I expect in a doctor's waiting room in Jerusalem? Edna gave up trying to find something interesting and returned the magazine to the rack.

Exploring the doctor's waiting room one step at a time, Sarah Leah toddled unsteadily around the crowded room. She stopped at the magazine rack, looked back at her mother, Miriam, and hesitated.

Miriam did not respond. She sat motionless in the chair next to Edna, staring at the painting of a desert on the wall opposite her.

Sarah Leah pulled a magazine off the rack and plopped down on the rug. She turned a few pages and shot an impish look at Miriam. Again, she had no response.

Oh! Oh! Edna thought. Now, *we're in for some real mischief.*

One page after another was torn out, crumpled, and then tossed aside. Other patients waiting their turn shifted uncomfortably in their seats and looked the other way. Miriam stared, unflinchingly, at the picture on the wall.

Sarah Leah took another magazine, destroyed it, and then another. Even if her mother screamed at her, it was better than her doing nothing. Then she took two or three at a time, tossing them in every direction.

Edna turned her head to her neighbor and stared, hoping to gain her attention. No response. No movement.

Trying to understand, Edna searched Miriam's pale face. Her bloodshot eyes and tight lips scarcely covered a well of sadness and desperation.

Edna caught herself suddenly, stopped staring, and sat upright. *What business is this of mine? Why should I care? What do the kids say? Keep cool? Don't get involved? They know what they're talking about.*

Edna returned to her magazine.

The toddler suddenly stopped what she was doing and a look of deep concentration appeared on her face. Her cheeks grew ruddy as she grunted. When she was finished, she wobbled over to her mother and pulled at her skirt. The pungent odor was inescapable. Miriam did not move.

Sarah Leah whined softly at first and then insistently.

Still, Miriam did not move.

Edna felt that she had no choice. She turned her head.

"Your baby needs a fresh diaper," she said sharply. *No chance of my being ignored now.*

Miriam turned her head slowly towards Edna to give her a withering look.

"So, diaper her!" Miriam returned Edna's sharpness with anger bordering on rage.

"Your daughter would like **you** to diaper her." Edna insisted.

Miriam looked at her baby. She was still pulling on her skirt. *She's right.* Miriam sighed.

"I am going to lose my turn." She said, stalling.

"I'm ahead of you. You won't lose your place."

Miriam rose slowly and picked Sarah Leah up.

"Are you next?" Miriam asked when they returned.

Sarah Leah, freshly diapered, returned to the magazine rack.

Edna nodded in assent. Then, without a word, she sighed and dabbed at her watery eyes with a tissue. Then she blew her nose.

Miriam was surprised. It was her turn to stare. *I guess misery loves company,* she thought. *We're both miserable. And, so? Does that make me any happier?*

Edna turned to her neighbor. "Why are you here?"

"I have pains in my chest that don't go away. I know that something's wrong. I've had lots of tests. They show nothing. Doctors don't know anything. I know that I'm very sick and I know that I'm dying. And nobody cares."

"What do you mean, nobody cares. Your baby cares. She needs you." Edna turned and looked into her eyes. "And what about your husband? Your parents?"

"My husband is a scholar. He's always busy studying. My mother died six months ago. She wants me to be with her." It was the young woman's turn to weep.

"Every mother wants her children to live long and healthy lives."

"I was too busy to go to her when she needed me. Now, I'll go."

Edna felt herself growing angry. "Now, you listen to me! Your mother wants you to live. And you want to live or you wouldn't be here. You have a beautiful little girl and she needs you.

"Your baby is making a mess all over the floor with those magazines. It's not nice. Tell her that it's not nice but tell her quietly and help her put them back. And, please, don't scream at her."

Obediently, Miriam walked over to the rack and replaced the magazines. Sarah Leah helped her. When they were finished, she placed her daughter on her lap, opened her purse, and gave her a ring of keys to play with.

She turned to Edna, "And why are *you* here?"

"I haven't been sleeping well at night. By the way, my name is Edna."

The young woman smiled. "I'm Miriam and my daughter's name is Sarah Leah."

Sarah Leah, bored with the keys, grabbed her mother's purse and overturned it. The small change tumbled out with a clatter and rolled across the floor. Miriam placed Sarah Leah on the floor while she bent down to pick up her money.

Edna retrieved a small mirror from her own purse and brought the child towards her. With a smile, she showed Sarah Leah her face in the mirror.

"Sarah Leah," Edna repeated softly. "What a pretty name and what a pretty little girl!" Edna smiled at her as she spoke. Sarah Leah smiled back.

"Edna," called a voice from across the room.

Sarah Leah whimpered when Edna left.

Edna's jacket remained on the back of her chair.

"What did the doctor say? How do you feel?" Miriam asked when Edna returned to pick up her jacket.

"He gave me a prescription, of course," Edna smiled. "Truthfully, I felt better when I went in. Doctors don't know anything, do they?"

Miriam's pale face turned pink. "I feel better now, too," she said.

The two women smiled at each other.

"I will watch Sarah Leah while you're having your turn," Edna offered. "Then we will have a nice cup of coffee."

Edna winked at Sarah Leah. "And a glass of milk and cookies as well."

"I'll have to pick up Moishele at nursery school but Simma, Baruch, Eli, and Tamara don't come home until later. OK, we'll sit with you while you're having your coffee. Thank you, but we brought our own thermos and cookies with us."

"Miriam." the voice called.

When Miriam disappeared down the hall, Edna looked after her. *Good Heavens! I counted six children. Are there more?*

"I'm a dressmaker, a good one. And I have a good business." Miriam shrugged. "I have to have a good business or we don't have money to eat or pay the rent. Sammy gets money from a grant for his Jewish studies but it's not enough. He spends all of his time learning at the yeshiva. Someday, should the All Powerful will it, he will be the head of his own yeshiva. When that happens, we will not have to worry about food on the table or a roof over our heads.

"But what about you?" Miriam asked Edna. "What about your husband? Your family?"

"My husband passed away last year. My two children are grown and married. My son and his family are in New York and my daughter and her family are in California. I miss them very much. We talk on the telephone but it is not the same."

Edna leaned over the table and looked into Miriam's eyes making sure that she had her attention.

"I am going to go to a formal wedding and I will need a brown velvet dress to match my silk shawl. I have been to all of the shops and found nothing," Edna paused meaningfully and leaned back in her chair.

"I'd make you a dress but I already have too much to do. My customers don't realize that sometimes I have to work until three or four o'clock in the morning to finish." Suddenly Miriam's face lit up as she looked at Edna. With a winning smile and pleading voice, she continued. "If I had help with the children I could do more. Baruch needs help with his English homework, Tamara doesn't understand fractions, and Simma, Moishele, and Sarah Leah need me to go to the park with them. Tamara and Eli are older but they're still only children and they need me to listen to them."

Edna looked at Sarah Leah and smiled broadly.

"What a coincidence! I don't have a thing to do this afternoon. And tomorrow. I have nothing to do either."

Miriam paused, took a deep breath, and released it slowly. "I think," she said, "I think that you have been sent from heaven! If you'll pay for the fabric, I'll make you a dress for the wedding for nothing."

"Everyone commented on my beautiful dress. I told my cousin Sally that she could not afford the price I paid. She believed me. What I meant was that Sally loves to go shopping, so it would be a hardship for her to give up her time to be with the children. I never liked to shop. So, for me the price is very low." Edna laughed. Sitting at the kitchen table between Baruch and Tamara, she hardly looked up as she spoke to Miriam. "Very low price, indeed!"

Miriam was pleased. "The children call you 'Savta' like they called my mother when she was still here. First Tamara started and then they all got the idea. They feel that they've a grandmother again. My friend, Pessy, asked me where I got you from and I told her that you're a present from *HaShem*. Maybe she believed me, maybe she didn't, but it's true."

After Sarah Leah was old enough to go to nursery school, Miriam realized, with a sigh, that she was carrying another child. *HaShem be blessed,* she thought, *He knows when our house needs another baby.*

Edna looked forward to the new baby. She found herself pleased with the world.

Edna, while helping Simma with her reading, was the first to notice that something was wrong.

"Why are your ankles so swollen?" She asked.

Surprised, Simma looked down at her feet. Not only were her ankles huge and overlapping the tops of her shoes but her shoes felt tight.

This is not something that happens to six year olds, Edna thought.

She walked over to Miriam to tell her.

"What do you mean Simma's kidneys stopped working?" Miriam was shocked. *What is this doctor telling us? I don't understand.*

"I don't understand. What did we do? What should we do?" Miriam's husband, Sammy, asked as they looked at each other in utter confusion.

The doctor spoke slowly and carefully. "Sometimes, these things happen. Nobody knows why. Simma will have to come to the hospital several days a week for treatment and she will have to stay for a few hours each time. It could take time, maybe weeks, maybe months, maybe even longer."

"Sweet words don't put food on the table." Miriam told Edna after a long day at the hospital.

Simma showed Edna all of her booty: The empty syringes the nurse had given her, the pictures she had drawn and the things that she had made in the hospital playroom.

"My clients say that they're sorry. They come to us, each of them, with hot soup and cooked chickens and rice still warm from the pot. They say that it's such a terrible thing to happen to such a nice little kid or to such a nice family. That, *Baruch HaShem*, Simma will be okay. It'll just take time and that I shouldn't worry.

"Then they go to another dressmaker! I can't blame them to tell the truth. They need dresses in time for weddings or suits for going on vacation and, even without sleep, I can't do everything. What am I going to do? I can't take my sewing machine to the hospital with me." Miriam turned her head away so Simma wouldn't see her tears.

Edna listened with one ear to Simma and with the other ear to Miriam.

"I will go with Simma to the hospital and I will find someone to take my place here until she is better. I was going to give Sammy and you an anniversary present of a weekend away at a nice hotel just for the two of you while I would take care of the children. This is a better idea."

Miriam laughed and cried at the same time, "From heaven! I must have done something good to deserve you.

After Simma was back in school full time and Miriam's baby was readying itself to be born, Edna woke one morning and decided that she would never again get out of bed. She drew her covers tightly around her and over her head as if to wrap herself in a cocoon, or perhaps, a shroud. She could see the bright sun rising high from her bedroom window. Edna did not move.

After a while she stretched out her arm to turn on the radio and listen to the news. *Murder and mayhem*, she thought. *Why did I bother? It is always the same. People murdered and maimed without reason.* She turned the radio off.

The biopsy was positive. Today is the day that I have to start planning for the rest of my life. I might just as well stay in bed.

Edna decided to go back to sleep. It did not happen. She turned on her side. That did not work. *Well, then*, she thought, *why would I want to stay in bed? I might dream. I might as well get up.*

While Edna was brushing her teeth, the phone rang. She smiled, despite herself. *Of course, the telephone would ring while I am in the bathroom. When else does the telephone ring?*

With a mouth full of toothpaste, Edna shuffled over to pick up the phone. *Whoever it is will hang up as soon as I get there. Why should this day be different?* This time, however, the caller stayed on the line. *You see,* she smirked to herself, *already something good happened today.*

Miriam was on the other end.

"No, thank you, but I don't need another thing." Edna said, not giving Miram a chance to talk. "Nothing. Not a dress, not a suit, nothing. I have a wardrobe fit for a queen. The rich and famous would envy me if they knew. Thank you for everything but I will not need anything anymore. The biopsy was positive."

After all, Edna thought, *what was Miriam to me or I to her? She made my clothing and I helped her with the children.*

"We had a business arrangement, nothing more."

Miriam gasped and, stunned, said nothing.

"We had a very nice arrangement while it lasted." Edna continued. "It was good for me. I wish that it could have lasted forever. But nothing lasts forever. You know that. I am happy that it lasted this long."

"I wish you and everybody in the family only the best. Goodbye." Edna was ready to replace the handset when she heard Miriam's shrill voice.

"What are you talking about?" Miriam screamed into the phone. "What nice arrangement? Good for you? What about me? What about the children? We need you like we need food in our stomachs or like we need blood in our veins. "What are you saying? You put a hole in my heart and you talk about arrangements? What arrangements?"

"A hole in your heart?" Edna was skeptical.

Miriam shrieked "A hole in my heart!"

"Just tell me why you called. Who's sick at home? Who has a problem? Where do you want to go? What do you want from me?"

"You tear me to pieces and then you ask me what I want from you. What are you doing to me? What are you doing about the biopsy?"

"I see the surgeon in a couple of hours."

"We'll go with you."

"We? Who are we?"

"Sarah Leah's nursery school is closed today. We'll be over in an hour." Miriam hung up.

Edna was just finishing her breakfast when Miriam and Sarah Leah arrived. Edna had been looking out of her window, watching the sun warm her flowers and dry what remained of the morning dew. A spider's web sparkled as if sprinkled with jewels and a bird flew right up to her sill chattering as if it had a story to tell and Edna could understand.

"Come, sit with me for a moment," Edna said invitingly. "We have time."

Miriam plumped down heavily on a chair and helped herself to a cup of coffee. Sarah Leah spied strawberries on the table and climbed onto Edna's lap. Edna laughed and gave her one.

"What a bandit!" she said.

"You never did tell me why you called," Edna told Miriam.

Edna laughed again as Sarah Leah stuck out her arm and asked for another. Edna gave it to her and then gave her a big hug and kiss and rocked her in her arms.

"My next door neighbor's son was on the bus yesterday when it was exploded and he's in the hospital." Miriam explained. "Don't get excited.

It could've been worse. With help from *HaShem*, he'll be okay. I wanted to know whether you would take care of Sarah Leah while I went to see him. I'll go tonight instead. It's better that I go tonight. I'm sure that right now he has more people around him than he needs or wants."

Edna looked at the clock.

"Time to go to the doctor."

She put Sarah Leah on the floor.

Miriam rose heavily from her chair. Edna put her arms around her and her unborn baby and kissed Miriam on the cheek.

"I love you." Edna said with tears of happiness welling in her eyes. "Thank you. Thank you very much."

A Family Visit

"Tuesday? You're coming this Tuesday? You're taking time off from the optical shop? The kids are off for Chanukah? Great. Pity about Gary working."

We were delighted to have our *Hassidic,* ultra-orthodox, niece, Rachel, and her children, four great-nieces and one great-nephew, aged 10 through 19, pay us a visit.

Rachel is an optician and Gary an optometrist. They have a shop in the Ramat Eshkol neighborhood in Jerusalem. In addition, Gary teaches optometry in the Hadassah College of Technology.

"We'll be sure to buy everything Badatz." What could be better than that? Wasn't Badatz the highest certification of kashrut with the most stringent code for kosher food, higher than certification by the Jerusalem rabbinate and higher than l'mehadrin certification?

We have no problem eating anything Rachel serves us. They are the ones with restrictions. Unless we plan carefully, they will eat or drink nothing in our home. Nothing but bottled water from a plastic cup. That would bother me. A lot.

"So far, we bought cookies from a Badatz bakery and rolls from another Badatz bakery." I was proud to tell Rachel. "Now what else do we prepare?" I was considering canned fish, cheeses, fruits, and vegetables. I was not prepared for the response.

"What kind of Badatz label?" Rachel was not pleased.

"What kind of Badatz label? What do you mean, what kind of Badatz label? You know, the kind of impressive squashed circle label." Something did not sound right.

"I'll give you to Aharon."

"What does it say inside the label?" Aharon, their sixteen year old yeshiva *bocher*, a student of religious studies and final voice on all things religious in their family, wanted to know.

"Hmm, what does it say?" I was apprehensive. "It says Badatz Beit Yosef."

"No good. No good from the beginning. Beit Yosef is not good but if you bought it already and in innocence there is nothing we can do about it."

"So, what is good?"

Aharon read off a list of *Badatz* certifications which are acceptable. I wrote them all down.

I looked at the list. Long. Impressive. "Aha. I see. Hmm. Looks like we're going to have pizza for lunch. I know from last summer that you would eat pizza made by a shop on Emek Refaim."

"Pizza shop? Pizza? Oh, oh, yes, yes. That one is good. That one we could eat."

"What about fruits and vegetables?" I asked.

"The fruits and vegetables must be bought from a Badatz greengrocer. There is one in the shuk near Jaffa Street."

No way was I going to *shlep* from one shop to another in the shuk near Jaffa Street looking for a greengrocer who sold Badatz label produce. And then the preparation. Something I would do after I unwrap, wash, and put them on the table would not be right. I could count on it. At the rate that we were going, it couldn't possibly be right.

"Please ask Ima to bring fruit and vegetables ready to put on plastic dishes."

Silence.

"We look forward to seeing you on Tuesday." Really, we did.

Hugs and kisses for all except for Aharon who kind of squeezed himself in while I was hugging and kissing Nechama. Since his Bar Mitzvah he would not touch or be touched by a woman. Not even by me. An old lady blood relative.

Time was, just after his Bar Mitzvah, that I would chase him around the living room until I caught him and claimed my dues.

Aharon is bigger and stronger now. I am older. I don't fight him anymore.

"Aharon! What a pleasure to see you! You've grown so tall!" I threw him a kiss.

Nechama, 19, works in a Hassidic *gan*, nursery school, part-time aide to the nursery school teacher and part-time secretary. Finished with high school and computer school except for classes one afternoon a week, she was delighted to find a paying job.

I would like for her to find a job using her talent with computers, She had put together a slide show for her sister's, Bayle, Bat Mitzvah, two years before, that was breathtaking.

Tamara, 18, is already a businesswoman. She runs a hairdressing salon from her bedroom and babysits in-between times.

Bayle, 14, is now in high school and a good student. Leah Hannah, 10, is also a good student. Bayle likes to write plays and Leah Hannah made all of the decorations for their *Succah*.

All of the children are warm, friendly, sensitive and kind. Rachel and Gary have much to be proud of.

We asked Aharon to say the blessings and light the Chanukah candles. We wanted to make sure that it was done right. Not that Ben doesn't do it right. He does it right. But, somehow, Aharon was, we were sure, just a little more right.

Everytime we see each other, we learn something new.

The pizza having been delivered, we washed hands and made blessings. Then we sat down to eat on plastic plates, cups, and utensils. But there was a problem.

In order to say the *Birkat Hamazon,* blessings after a meal, a blessing must be made over a piece of bread before eating. Pizza dough is not considered bread. We had sliced bread in the freezer which could be defrosted in the microwave. Aharon shook his head. The bread would have to be between two pieces of aluminum foil. No way! Foil would set the microwave on fire. Each of the children ate a slice of bread, frozen. They had forgotten to ask whether or not the bread was Badatz or what kind of Badatz it was.

I mentioned while we ate that we had friends who had a grandson who was nice, bright, handsome and was about to earn his *smichah,* his ordination, as a *Lubavatcher* rabbi, and was also young and single. I had told our friends, more than once, about our two older, beautiful, and talented great-nieces. I expected to arouse interest in our niece and in at least one of our great-nieces. I did not.

Several of Nechama's and Tamara's friends are married. One of Tamara's friends had a baby a few months ago. She's seventeen years old. Her friend's mother is thirty-four years old.

"We are not Lubavatcher Hassidim. We are *Litvisher* Hassidim." Rachel contributed

"I did not know that. I had no idea that you were not Lubavitch. Does that mean Lubavatcher Hassidim do not marry Litvisher Hassidim?"

They shook their heads in assent.

Would that be a mixed marriage? I almost asked the question but did not. The answer was obvious.

We hugged and kissed again as the children left. Except for Aharon, of course.

"We must see each other again soon." I shouted into the air as they left to catch the elevator.

"Of course, of course. *L'Hitraot!* We'll see you soon." was the answer.

Love transcends.

The Experiment

It's an experiment. Anat slowed the car as she approached the area assigned by the school where Liora and Rivkah, hand in hand, were waiting for her. Anat parked at the curb and got out of the car.

Anat looked down at Rivkah and tried to calm herself. *We knew it wouldn't be easy. We knew before we came that it was an experiment and it might not work. But,* Anat turned her head to the side and took a deep breath, *give me strength. She stinks! When did she last take a bath? And her clothes. Does she ever change them? Cheap rags! And filthy!*

Anat hesitated and then spoke softly in a clear and even voice. "Rivkah, would you like to come home with us and stay for supper? Liora and you could do your homework together. Liora would be happy to help you if you want. But, first, I must call your Ima and ask permission for you to come with us. What is your telephone number?"

Rivkah's hand lay relaxed in Liora's grasp. She looked up at Anat. "We don't have a telephone."

"Oh, then we have go to your home and ask permission."

"Only Savta is home. Ima works all day at the laundry. Can Savta give per-mish-yon, too?

Anat smiled at Rivkah, a wide and benevolent smile, to put Rivkah at ease and to prove that the experiment was working.

Liora also smiled, not letting go of her new friend's hand. "Please, Ima, pu-lease! Rivkah is smart. You'll see."

"Where do you live, Rivkah?"

Rivkah pointed with her free hand.

Of course! Right in the heart of the industrial area slum!

Anat opened the door to the back seats of her car and the girls piled in dragging their schoolbags behind them.

The brave experiment was working! Lovely! Anat made herself comfortable behind the steering wheel. *It was up to us to change the terrible reputation of the city. They built homes for us young, professional families but no new schools or synagogues so that we would have to interact with the poor people who live here and improve their lives. We would be pioneers. It sounded so good. Many of us, doctors, lawyers, and successful business people, never saw a really poor person in our lives. Or smelled one, either,* Anat sat up straight. She was determined to make a difference!

Rivkah, Liora, and Anat walked up a dark, dirty stairway that reeked of cabbage, garlic and burnt onions. Rivkah opened the door with her key.

Savta's large frame lay immobile on her bed in the room that also served as kitchen, dining room, and living room. Her bloated abdomen formed a mound standing out from the rest of her prostrate body. Startled by strangers, she pulled her blanket up as far as she could but it would not cover her face. Without a word, she turned her head towards the wall. The room reeked of urine and other unpleasant odors.

Rivkah sat on the edge of the bed and put her arm around her Savta. "Savta, Savta, it's alright! It's only Liora and her Ima. I told you about Liora. They want me to go home with them. I'm going to do homework with Liora and then we'll eat and then Liora's Ima will bring me home."

Savta turned her face to Rivkah and looked directly into her eyes. "Who are these people? Are they going to teach you strange ways? Can you trust them?"

"It's alright, Savta. I know that it will be alright. I'll be home before Ima."

Anat came close to the bed. "We'll take good care of Rivkah. She will have supper with us and then we will bring her right home."

Savta stared at Liora and Rivka as they walked out. She had nothing else to say.

I'll go through Liora's clothing as soon as we get home. There's a bag of stuff that we were going to give away. I can give Rivkah the entire bag and, maybe, another bag as well. While they're doing their homework, I'll go next door to Chavah and see if she has large size clothing for Savta. Chavah is a big woman. Wait until I tell her!

What do I have in the refrigerator? In the freezer? We'll help Rivkah carry everything home.

The experiment is working! I can't wait to tell everyone.

"You'll have something to eat and drink before you do your homework." Anat ushered the girls to the kitchen table. She brought them milk, cookies, and fruit. *Whatever they leave behind, Rivkah can take home with her.*

"Liora will be happy to help you with your homework, Rivkah." Anat gave Rivkah an especially broad smile. "And, afterwards, you can both play until supper is ready." Anat turned towards Liora. "Maybe you'll teach Rivkah to play checkers like Aba taught you."

"I think Rivkah would rather watch a movie." Liora preferred a movie.

Anat frowned, just a little. "Oh well, we'll discuss it again after you finish your homework, I would really prefer that you teach Rivkah checkers or some other game."

Anat went to work immediately. She found the bag of old clothing, *I won't even bother going through it. If they can't use all of it, well, others will, I'm sure.* Then, as she had already planned, Anat went through Liora's closet, starting methodically at one end, going from one hanger at a time, removing everything Liora had not worn for a while and would soon be discarded. When she was finished, she had another large bag of clothing.

Then Anat went next door to Chavah in search of clothing for Savta. Her excitement was contagious. Chavah also rummaged through her closet and another bag was promptly filled. In addition, Chavah donated a cake she had just baked. Anat felt satisfied looking over the pile of things that she had put together for Rivkah. Now she would see how far the girls progressed with their homework.

"Ima, Rivkah is so smart! She helped me with my homework and now I understand everything. Do you know that Rivkah reads books? She just read me a story."

Anat, taken aback, said nothing. The broad smile slowly vanished. "Did you finish your homework?"

"Oh, Ima, with Rivkah to help me, we finished right away. She's so smart."

"Do you really read books, Rivkah? Liora and you are only in second grade. Does someone give you books?"

It was Rivkah's turn to smile. "I go to the library all of the time. It's so nice and warm there in the winter and so cool in the summer. I take books off of the shelf and read them there. I used to go to the baby books but now I can read real books. Sometimes the librarian shows me which books to read. Sometimes I take books home. Especially for Shabbat."

"You see how smart Rivka is, Ima. Now I don't have to worry about not understanding my homework anymore. Rivkah could even do it for me. I am so happy to have Rivkah for a friend."

"Now, that's lovely, isn't it? Liora will never have to worry about her homework anymore." Anat tried to smile once again. She didn't succeed. Her voice had a chill to it. "Your Ima must be very proud of you."

"Ima said that she's jealous of me. She always wanted to read but she always had to work. She never went to school. I help Ima when I can. She's always tired. Sometimes I read to Savta when she wants to listen. Do you want me to read to you, too?"

Anat was horrified. "No! Thank you. Perhaps some other time."

"Why not, Ima?" Liora was puzzled.

Anat said nothing for a moment and then smiled a big, broad smile. once again. "I would love for you to read to me but supper is almost ready and as soon as Aba is home, we'll have supper together and then we'll take you home, Rivkah. In the meantime, you could watch a movie if you like."

"Could Rivkah come tomorrow again?" Liora was eager.

Anat hesitated. *We know nothing about this girl. We have no idea who she associates with in her neighborhood, if you could call it that. They have drugs, disease, and even prostitution. What kind of stupid experiment did they plan? So much for stupid experiments!*

"Not tomorrow, Liora." *What excuse could I give?*

The Honored Guest and
the Distinguished Host

Fantasy Inspired by the Welcome Given to Pope Benedict XVI in Honor of his Historic Visit to Israel, May 2009, by the President of Israel, Shimon Peres.

Only Jerusalem could have such a day. A golden sun set in a violet-blue sky was cooled by a caressing breeze. Smiles greeted smiles as strangers passed one another in the street. A Jerusalem day cheered the soul and warmed the heart.

The honored guest from Germany sat in the seat reserved for him at the formal reception in the distinguished host's official home. The reception was held in the garden, made warm and bright with spring blossoms. A choir of schoolgirls dressed in white serenaded him sweetly with songs of Israel and its longing for peace.

The honored guest smiled.

When the girls finished, the distinguished host spoke. He spoke of the honored guest's mission to Israel as one of peace.

The honored guest leaned back in his chair and regarded his host.

A Jew! He thought to himself. *A Polish Jew at that! The damned of the damned!*

The honored guest snickered imperceptibly and, then, with a start, remembered who he was and where he was. He sat up straight and smiled.

What did they tell us in the Hitler youth? They told us that the blood of the Jews must run in the streets. And it ran in the streets. I was there.

Is it a dream? Am I dreaming? We killed as many Jews as we could. We murdered them one at a time and many all at once.

In his imagination, the honored guest addressed his distinguished host. *How many of your grandparents, parents, brothers, sisters, cousins, and friends did we slaughter? Do you know? Do you remember?*

The honored guest stared at his distinguished host. Slowly, feelings of familiarity, as if they had met before, grew into recognition. *Yes, I remember you now. We are old now but we were children once.*

Franz and I were coming home from a Hitler Youth meeting when we saw you coming from school. You were alone. Franz shouted to me that it's a Yid and that we have to go after you. We looked at each other. You were one. We were two. We curled our fingers into tight fists and hurried towards you. We were ready to have our fun. But before we could reach you, you went into a house.

We looked for you after our next meeting and you were coming home from school again. This time you were with Herr Spiegel, the football player. Herr Spiegel was also a Jew but he was big and strong. We decided to wait until next time.

The next time there were nine of us and we went to look for you. Franz had his bicycle and a piece of wood with nails in it. You had four Yid friends with you. Franz put the piece of wood in his basket, mounted his bicycle, put his head down and charged. Your friends ran away. He thought that you would run away, too, but you stood there, feet apart, and stared at Franz as he charged. Franz had his piece of wood ready. As soon as Franz came close and was going to hit you, you grabbed the handlebars of his bicycle and twisted them around. The bicycle fell over and Franz fell on top of it.

Franz started to cry and I helped him to get up. He cried harder when he saw that his bicycle was bent. I told the others to let you alone. It was enough. You walked away with your friends. I never saw you again. Until now.

The honored guest leaned back in his seat.

Now I am old. And I am tired. I have lived my life. Within me only my memories live.

What is there left for me to do?

The distinguished host was concluding his welcoming speech. He looked expectantly at his honored guest.

"In you, we see a great spiritual leader, a potent bearer of the message of peace to this land and to all others."

The honored guest's turn had come. He lumbered up to the microphone, stood as straight as he could, and spoke.

"The Jewish people have suffered the terrible consequences of ideologies that threaten the dignity of every human being."

The distinguished host smiled with satisfaction. *So far, so good.* He sat down and made himself comfortable. He could now look unseeingly at his honored guest and think his own thoughts and dream his own dreams.

How many years has it been? I knew you as soon as I saw you. The bright blue eyes and thin lips. Had I been torn and bleeding you would have done nothing to stop them. You were a Hitler Youth with the rest of them.

The first time I saw you was when I was coming home from school and I looked up to see your friend and you coming towards me with your fists clenched. I opened the door nearest me and went inside. An old lady lived there and, when she saw me, was going to scream. When I pointed to the window she looked out and saw the two of you in your uniforms. Then she understood. When you passed, I left.

The next time Herr Spiegel was at the school and I asked him to walk with me because I had questions to ask him. I was happy that he was with me when you came again. I knew, then, that I would see you again and again until my body was broken. Then you would be satisfied.

After that I asked four friends to walk with me. I told them that there were only two of you and that the five of us would be enough. When we saw that you were nine and that you had a bicycle, they backed off. I had no choice. I knew that you would not go away. When I saw the bicycle I knew what I had to do.

For all of the years I did not see you again until now.

The honored guest was still speaking.

"The Assyrians, the Philistines, and the Romans, all oppressors of the Jews, are no more. Neither are the Nazis. My friends in the Hitler Youth were killed during the war.

"You have persisted with God's help because of your ingenuity and bravery. With God's help you will always be here and with God's help you will have peace with your neighbors.

"We will help you fight anti-Semitism and unreasoning hatred and violence. It is God's will."

The distinguished host rose and shook the hand of the honored guest.

"I believe," he said, "That dinner is ready."

The two old men walked together, side by side, arm in arm to the dining room.

The Miracle

Little Moishee pecked unthinkingly at the keyboard with one finger. His chin lay in the cup of his hand propped up on its elbow beside the computer. *Homework,* he thought. *Even in Israel in the middle of a war with the terrorist driven Hamas. Even here in the* miklat, *the secure room, where we spend most of our time, with sirens blasting away when we least expect them and missiles and rockets flying all over the place, I'm still supposed to do my homework.*

Little Moishee's homework assignment coupled with his lesson was sent by email to his entire class. His teacher was determined to not let her students fall behind even when the school was closed. She did not want the children exposed to danger. The lesson and homework assignment lay neatly beside the computer. He knew what he was supposed to do. He just did not feel like doing it.

Red alert! Red alert! Missiles sighted! Go to the *miklat* immediately!

The sirens and bullhorns blasted their terrible messages for everyone to hear.

He sighed but did not move. *I'm so lucky, Ima keeps telling me. I don't have to go to a* miklat. *I'm in one already. So is Leahle sitting in a corner reading a book. So is Ima doing her work on her computer. She hardly ever goes into the office anymore. Even Aba does most of his work in our garage. He arrived before the sirens and bullhorn stopped and closed the door behind him.*

Only Avram is missing. Little Moishee glanced at the steel shutter on the lone window, the especially heavy steel door, and the special light set in the middle of the ceiling. *I guess we're lucky to have a* miklat *right here. I wish Avram were here, too.*

Last week, when a rocket hit our roof and made a big hole in it, our neighbors told us how lucky we were because we didn't get hurt. They didn't get hurt either. They were safe in their own safe rooms.

I bet that Avram isn't in a miklat. *Wherever he is, he has only his rifle, uniform, and helmet to protect him. I know, too, that, wherever he is, there are guns and missiles aimed at him. Shlomo, Avram's friend, from around the corner, is home from the hospital. Ima said that it will take a long time before he will be better. Some soldiers get killed. I know. I know, too, that Avram is in the army to keep us safe here, at home. When I'm bigger, I'll be in the army, too.*

Boom!

A missile made contact. Everyone shuddered. Nobody said a word.

All Clear!

The siren sounded a few minutes later. Aba opened the door and everybody, except for Little Moishee, went outside to see what damage had been done. After everyone looked at the gaping hole in the wall of the Levy's kitchen, making it unusable for at least a week, Aba went back to work in the garage. Ima returned briefly to shut down her computer and then went to the kitchen to make something to eat. Leahle went to help her.

Little Moishee was left alone in the miklat. He remained in the same place, in the same position, pecking away at the keyboard. With his eyes half closed, thoughtlessly, he typed with one finger the word "G-o-l-e-m."

Bing!

Huh! Little Moishee picked his head up and looked around. *What was that?*

Bing! Bing! Bing!

Little Moishee sat up straight and looked around the room. He was alone. *Where did the noise come from?* He went back to his position by the computer. *Hey! Something was moving on the computer screen. What's that? It looks like a man dancing around dressed in a white tunic and a long, wide, and dark blue cloak. He smiled at Little Moishee.*

"Who are you?" Little Moishee asked out loud.

"A Golem. You asked for me. At your service." The man on the screen bowed.

"A Golem on a computer screen? What kind of Golem are you? A Golem is big and strong and helps Jews. What good are you on a computer screen?"

Boing!

The man in the white tunic jumped out of the screen and stood tall. He towered over Little Moishee.

"I am here because you need my help. How may I help you?"

"I want to see Avram. I miss him and I'm afraid." He started to cry. The Golem's question unleashed tears stored for so long that even Little Moishee did not know how deeply they had been hidden.

The Golem stretched his arm and drew Little Moishee towards him, enveloping him completely in his dark blue cloak. At the same time, Little Moishee felt as if he were spinning, slowly at first and then faster and faster. When he caught his breath and peeped beyond the cloak, he saw Avram. He automatically stretched his arm towards him.

"Avram! Are you alright? I miss you."

Avram was crouched alongside a wall, his rifle pointed straight at the doorway to the United Nations building opposite him. Slowly a crying boy emerged, pushed by a man in civilian clothes, clutching the boy's clothing at the neck in one hand and holding a cocked pistol aimed directly at Avram in the other.

"Avram! Avram! Watch out! He's going to shoot you! Shoot him! Shoot him!" Little Moishee screamed frantically.

"He can't shoot. He doesn't want to hurt the boy. And, he can't hear you." The Golem held Little Moishee within the cloak.

With all his strength, Little Moishee pushed himself free of the Golem, grabbed a rock and threw it at the terrorist. It glanced off his forehead, stunning him. He released the child. The boy ran away. Avram aimed at the terrorist and then shot and killed him with one bullet.

Once more, the Golem enveloped Little Moishee in his cloak and he felt as if he was spinning faster and faster. He closed his eyes. When he opened them he was back in the *miklat*.

The Golem released Little Moishee and rewrapped his cloak around himself so that he covered himself entirely except for his face. He bowed once more to Little Moishee and then jumped back into the computer screen. Waving goodbye, he covered his face and disappeared.

Little Moishee dropped himself down into the seat in front of the computer and took a deep breath.

I have to tell everyone I saw Avram. He started to rise and, then, slowly stopped in mid-air, and sat down again. *Who would believe me? A Golem from the computer? Ima would feel my forehead to see if I had temperature. Aba would yell at me, accusing me of trying to get out of doing my homework. Leahle would giggle. Why do girls giggle so much? Nobody would believe me. To be honest, if Leahle told me the same story, I wouldn't believe her either.*

"Where were you? Why didn't you come?" Leahle burst into the *miklat* and shouted. "Ima sent me to get you to come to the table to eat. And I've been calling you and calling you. Why didn't you answer?"

Leahle turned to look at the computer screen. "I don't believe it. You still haven't done your homework. Aba is going to give it to you good and you deserve it!" Leahle was working herself into a frenzy and was not about to give up. "Avram is out there fighting and risking his life for all of us and you don't even care."

Little Moishee opened his eyes wide and his mouth followed. He shut them both and said nothing.

When Avram, safe and sound but exhausted, arrived home on leave before Shabbat, he was given a hero's welcome. Ima hugged and kissed him and then cried for joy. And, of course, it goes without saying, set a place for Avram at the table and emptied the refrigerator. Aba gave Avram a big hug that seemed to last forever. He turned his head so that we should not see his tears. Leahle and Little Moishee gave him hugs and, of course, Little Moishee punched him on the shoulder. Avram punched him back. They were brothers.

After dinner, everyone turned to Avram to say something. Anything. Not long after he came home, he walked over to visit Shlomo. He said nothing when he came back. Now, they wanted to hear.

"*HaShem* was looking out for me." Avram started, haltingly. His entire body helped his mouth tell the story.

"We were fired on from inside the UN building. The Hamas stopped at nothing. They knew that we respect the UN for its neutrality and leave it alone as we leave hospitals, schools, and mosques alone. But they gave us no choice. They were firing at us and we had to go in. I had my rifle trained on the door. Our commander shouted through his bullhorn telling the terrorists to get out. We weren't taking chances. A terrorist started out. I aimed my rifle in case he was going to shoot. I wanted to shoot first. Then I saw that he pushed a crying boy out ahead of himself. He looked like Little Moishee. I hesitated. He took aim."

Avram hesitated. He muttered something under his breath and then continued.

"HaShem was with me. The terrorist's head jerked suddenly and he lost control. The boy ran away. I shot the terrorist.

"Others came out but they came with their hands in the air. When we went inside, we saw a stockpile of missiles and explosives. HaShem was with all of us on that day.

"From now on, if anybody asks if I believe in miracles, I will say "Yes.""

Little Moishee said nothing but he knew that for all of the years of his life, he would remember.

Crabby Old People

"Why would you want to travel with all those crabby old people? They can't hear, see, or walk. Especially walk. And you're going on a three day trip with them? You're out of your mind."

Diane was exasperated with her mother. She was frequently exasperated especially with her mother.

"It's a study vacation," Evelyn answered. "We're going with the American Jewish War Veterans in Israel. Is it their fault that there haven't been any American wars for a while and that there aren't any new veterans? We'll be on a kibbutz to learn about the environment while we're having three meals a day and the beds made. Is that so terrible? And what do you mean, all *those* old people? Since when did you stop looking me in the face and up and down? You didn't notice?"

Diane screwed up her face as if to say she did not agree but said nothing.

So what's there to say?

"So some of us can see better or hear better or walk better than others." Evelyn continued. "So? So not everybody's perfect. So what?"

Evelyn snapped her suitcase shut. She was finished. Now she could plop down on the easy chair while waiting for the taxi.

"Who knows, maybe I'll meet Mr. Charming and we'll trip the light fantastic."

"Trip the light fantastic?" Diane giggled. "That alone dates you. Mr. Charming had better be able to see his way through his cataracts or the light fantastic will not be the only thing you'll be trippng over."

Three canes, no walkers. Evelyn looked around the meeting room. She had a schedule in her hand and was waiting for the orientation to begin. *One of the canes was long and thin. The kind the blind use. Double whammy!*

"We all have schedules so there will be no discussion about what we're doing or where we're going at any time. According to schedule the bird sanctuary is our first stop.

"We will make our first pit stop here and board the bus in fifteen minutes." Charles, the group leader, was acting the army officer he had once been.

"Aren't we all going to introduce ourselves to each other first?" Ella, to whom the cane for the blind belonged, objected to Charles' abruptness.

"We each have name tags. We're late."

"Fifteen minutes for the toilet isn't enough. Not for the women, at least. It'll take at least that long to wait on line." Paula, heavy and slow moving, even with her cane, knew that she would be last.

Charles' face spoke for him.

Crabby! Why? Don't we have enough problems? Evelyn looked around. *Look at that! He's setting the tone. There's more than one sour face in the crowd.* She frowned, adding her face to the rest.

"We will have to change our plans in order to cut costs. A lot of people cancelled out unexpectedly in the last week and that caused a lot of problems. We will have a box lunch instead of going to a restaurant. We don't want to overrun our budget." Charles' statement was flat, unapologetic.

The changes were not well received.

"Other people cancelled out. Not us." Eddie was indignant. "Why are we paying for the problems other people cause?" "I have half a mind to ask for a refund. We're being taken advantage of," Sam chimed in.

Paula had to have her say. "We paid up and look how we're being thanked."

"I was here first and I want to be served first," Eddie shouted at Paula in the dining room later that day. Paula, who was nearly deaf, had pushed herself up front.

Paula stopped short and stared at Eddie. "You can be served first, second, and last as far as I'm concerned. And you know what you could do with it when you have it!" She walked off with her head in the air.

Deep sighs came from within the group.

"I don't like your political insinuations! You've just insulted our government and our prime minister." Sam stood up. His face turned red. "That's not what you're here to discuss! You're here to discuss water conservation!" Sam banged his fist on the table, waking two people. Everyone else jumped.

Sam's voice rose to a shout. "I don't want your politics! Who's your boss? I'm going to report you!"

Evelyn groaned. *This lecture was really interesting. Why did Sam find it necessary to blow his top over a stupid remark? Couldn't he have waited until the end and then voiced his objections privately to the speaker?*

Evelyn turned to Ella. "Maybe my daughter, Diane, was right. Just too many crabby old people."

Ella smiled. "Not at all. No. Not at all. People are people after all. Young and old. A sour person can make everyone sour. But a sweet person can turn everyone sweet again." She winked with her blind eye.

"We'll see." She laughed at her own joke. "You'll see after supper tonight what a little sweetness can do."

Little discussion took place that night in the dining room during supper. Nobody knew what a simple conversation could lead to.

Ella broke the silence during desert time when, unasked, she started to hum. She hummed quietly at first and then a couple of people smiled and hummed along with her. She hummed louder. More people joined in. Someone started to sing. The tunes were old, tried and true, loved by all.

Ella stood up, tapped her cane to the center of the room, and sang out loud for all to hear. Her voice was clear and her song was joyful. Everyone joined in. Passersby joined in and her audience grew. Even Charles bellowed, off-key, drowning out the timid.

Music filled the dining room and the night air. Windows opened all over the kibbutz and everyone, two years old and older, sang. Some songs were sung for the first time. Many were off key. No matter. Radios and televisions were turned off, unneeded.

The joyous singing continued until the dining room manager reluctantly blinked the lights, signaling that it was time to say, "Goodnight," and to retire for the night.

"May I guide you? The ground is damp and slippery." Sam put Ella's hand in his as they left the dining room.

Ella smiled, grateful for the warmth of his hand and steadying support.

Eddie offered Paula his arm. They walked out arm in arm.

Evelyn took Charles' arm. They smiled at each other.

So, Prince Charming doesn't always come on his own. Sometimes he has to be helped along.

So, what does Diane know? Evelyn felt triumphant. *I can't wait to tell her.*

Souvenirs

"Almost three days of travel and not a single souvenir."

Fork in hand, I attacked the full plate in front of me with gusto. Our educational excursion from Jerusalem to the northern area around Natanya was coming to an end and all was for nothing. How would our grandchildren know that we were in interesting places and did interesting things if we would not bring back something tangible for them, like: A boomerang from Australia, tulips from Holland, or a cowboy hat from Texas.

Ordinarily the tour bus hardly warmed itself in winter or cooled itself in summer when my search for souvenirs began. Actually I did, once, find souvenirs on the first day of our trip and enjoyed the rest of the trip carefree. But that was unusual.

The museum of the city of Hadera was made all the more interesting by our guide, a highly educated woman who was eighty-six years old and the youngest daughter of original settlers. She pointed to the photographs of her family members on the walls of the orientation room of the museum and told us of the hardships they had to endure. As if we were there, we could smell the stench coming from the swamps which bred hoards of malaria carrying mosquitos. We felt her horror as one family member after another succumbed to chills and high fever. Only half her family survived the ravages of the disease. We felt the first settlers' frustration with the Turkish rulers of the land who refused for six years to allow the settlers to drain the swamps or to build. We took pride with them as they drained the swamps and rid the breeding ground for disease. We took pride with our guide in the Jewish community which grew and prospered from its very primitive beginnings.

"What, no literature? No picture postcards? Not even ballpoint pens with the name of the city on them? What kind of a tourist trap is this?" I had my priorities in evaluating a public institution.

And so it was with Utopia—the Orchid Park. We walked up, down and around looking at every color, every size, and every shape orchid displayed on slopes and in corners singly and in groups. We listened to a talk on carnivorous plants and passed a few small potted ones around, not daring to even lightly touch any part of the plant. We had been warned by our lecturer and emerged with all of our extremities intact.

"How come the staff wears attractive black T-shirts with the Utopia logo on their right shoulders? Why aren't there T-shirts of every size and, perhaps, every color, for every family member?" I lectured two of the guides on economics and public relations. They shrugged their shoulders. I could have also mentioned that I would have been spared the agony of continuing my search for souvenirs.

And at the Technoda, an educational center for technology and science located in the midst of a new industrial park that housed large, attractive, and modernistic corporate buildings. (Who would have expected an industrial park to rise from infectious swampland during the space of one person's lifetime?) While not a school itself, the Technoda provided enrichment programs for visiting classes from the first grade through high school seniors. Gifted children were offered residential programs lasting several weeks.

Their equipment was impressive, including an igloo-like inflatable planetarium which could seat twenty people at one time and show the sky exactly as a planetarium of much larger proportions did. We sat in total darkness in a circle on the perimeter of the igloo. Then the two headed camera unique to a planetarium showed a star-lit sky and I felt as if I were sitting in the middle of a desert with an endless sky above me. What a surprise when the presentation was over and the igloo was suffused with light to find myself back again in a structure just large enough to seat twenty!

"What, nothing for sale? No books? No toys which demonstrate scientific principles?" I summed up our visit to the impressive Technoda in frustration. "How would our granddaughters know where we went if we did not bring back souvenirs?"

Finally, happiness and joy, the last site we visited, a chocolate factory, sold souvenirs. The chocolate was handmade, expensive and made locally. Also, the chocolate could be purchased in small packages. We bought like drunkards in a winery.

"We have something for you," we told our two youngest granddaughters, eight-year old Talia and two-year old Jenna. When Jenna was one year and a half, she tasted chocolate for the first time. For three days after, she walked around the house wailing, "More chocolate!" Her genes were not to be denied.

Our granddaughters listened carefully. "We have for everybody in the family—chocolate!" They laughed and hugged each other. Their pure, unadulterated joy was a moment to be cherished.

IRENE

Irene

Sharpispaduck, Hungary was where I, Irene, was born and maybe where I will die. Why do I think that I might die there? I will tell you why. Because I am 91 years old and next week I am going to take my two children and two of my ten grandchildren to Sharpispaduck, Hungary, to show them where I was born and where I grew up.

I am going to show them my parents' home with its big garden where all of the Jews who came back from the camps came to eat Shabbat dinner. I was the first to come back and I cooked Shabbat dinner for everybody.

When I came back from Auschwitz to the town where I grew up and to the house where I was born, I opened the door to my parents' house, the house with the big garden and rooms enough for two parents, four children, and two servants, I told the people who were living there that they had twenty-four hours to leave. The next day I went home.

I was there when Yitzhak, the youngest of my three brothers, came back. Our parents did not come back, just the children, and not all of the children. One of my brothers did not come back.

I was the oldest of four children and sixteen years old when Yitzhak was born. He was the most beautiful baby in Sharpispaduck. I was so proud when I would wheel him to the park in his carriage and everybody would come to look at his pink, round, and smiling face. Our neighbor, Alice, had a baby the same age but he did not compare to Yitzhak. I felt a little sorry for Alice and she was very jealous. The first time we saw each other, after I came back, she hid her face.

The Jews who came back were given good jobs and I was given a good job in the office of the flour mill and I was satisfied. After

Auschwitz, I did not think to get married and when Mr. Danzicer came to talk with me I told him this. But he asked me again and he asked his friends to talk with me.

"Do you think that you are too beautiful to marry Mr. Danzicer?" one of his friends asked. "I assure you that his wife was ten times more beautiful than you."

"Mr. Danzicer thinks that I am beautiful? After Auschwitz, he thinks that I am beautiful?"

So, we were married.

Mr. Danzicer owned three vineyards and a wine cellar and we had servants even before the children came. But I wanted to leave Hungary. My brother, Yitzhak, had left and I wanted to leave also. Mr. Danzicer said that we would leave right away if we could take the vineyards and wine cellar with us.

"We will leave, Irene," he said. "But it will take time."

Then the Communists came and everybody had to go to the town clerk to register his property. So I went, too, to the town clerk like everybody else. The clerk and I recognized each other. When it was my turn, he called me a dirty Jew and I called him a dirty Nazi and I told him that he was an even worse Communist than he was a Nazi and I spit in his face.

When I went home and told Mr. Danzicer, he said, "Now, Irene, you will have your wish. We leave tonight."

We went from Hungary with our two children and one suitcase in the middle of the night and left everything behind.

There is nobody in Sharpispaduck, Hungary whom I know. My brother, Yitzhak, is now seventy-five years old and is a husband, father, grandfather, and great-grandfather and does not want to go back. My son, Shlomo, wants to see the vineyards and the wine cellar. I have the deeds. Shlomo can go without me.

Maybe we will meet a son or daughter or grandson or granddaughter who will remember. Maybe Alice's son is there. Maybe there is still a familiar stone or brick that will help me tell my story to my children. When I will not be here anymore *they* will remember.

The Vase

"But *Ima* it's such a pretty crystal vase. Look how nice it will look on the shelf next to the books. Why would you put it in the sack for old things that we don't need anymore?"

Katya turned the little vase around and around in her hands, watching the crystal shine blue, yellow, and orange in the light.

"Look at the label. It was made in Germany."

"But, Ima, it was a gift from our next door neighbors from their trip to Europe. They wanted to thank you for making sure that their apartment was alright when they were away. They're nice people and they like you." Katya put the vase on the shelf. "That's where it belongs."

Irene made a mental note to put the vase back in its box and in the sack as soon as Katya went to school.

Katya knew that she was born in Hungary after the Second World War. She knew that she did not have grandparents or many uncles, aunts, or cousins like her friends did. She knew but she did not understand. How could she have known about Auschwitz?

Irene had been a beautiful young woman when she was sent to the camp. She was part of a group of only beautiful young women. After the war, they were no longer beautiful or young. They went home no longer young or beautiful.

Mr. Danzicer also went home alone. His wife did not come back.

Soon after, Irene and Mr. Danzicer were married.

After Katya and her brother were born, the Communists came to Hungary. When they took control of Hungary, Irene and Mr. Danzicer took their children, Shlomo and Katya, and one suitcase in the middle of the night and left the country.

Katya learned Jewish history in school. And she learned about the Second World War. The Germans, Italians, and Japanese started a war and the Americans won. She also learned there was a *Shoah*, Holocaust, and that Jews suffered. She learned but she did not understand.

When Katya came home from school, she took the vase out of the bag for old things, out of the box it came in, and put it back on the shelf.

"I don't understand you." She said to her mother. "It's just a pretty crystal vase. So what if it was made in Germany. It's still pretty."

Irene said nothing. As soon as Katya was out of the house, the crystal vase went back to the garage.

As soon as Katya came home, the crystal vase was put back on the shelf.

The crystal vase became a game between Irene and Katya. After a while, the vase would go into the sack in the morning and return to the shelf in the afternoon. Neither Irene nor Katya thought about what they were doing. It was just something that was done. It was done, that is, until Katya, having nothing better to do, watched a movie on television about the Shoah.

The movie detailed the horror and cruelty of the Germans in carrying out mass deportations, the debasement and the dehumanization of Jews. It also detailed the starvation, the wanton murders, and the ovens. It left little to the imagination. Katya watched in stupefied horror from beginning to end.

Katya sat for a while when it was over. Then she went to the kitchen to see Irene.

"I didn't understand. You didn't tell me."

Irene shrugged. "What was there to tell a child?"

The next morning when the pretty crystal vase made in Germany was taken off the shelf and put into the sack, it stayed there.

Jerusalem 2003: Irene's Day

Here it is Wednesday and the children are coming for Shabbat. Irene looked at her watch. *It is 8:30AM and I asked Rutie to come at 8:00AM. So, I will go without her.* Irene checked her appearance in the mirror before leaving. *I am very good company for myself.*

Before Irene turned her key in the lock, she could hear the telephone ringing. It was her son, Shlomo. "Where were you? I was in Jerusalem in your apartment two hours ago and I've been calling you ever since."

"What do you mean 'Where was I?' I went out. I had things to do."

"The agency called me. Your helper, Rutie, came this morning and rang your bell. You didn't answer. She called the agency and the agency called me. I called Uncle Yitzhak. I thought maybe you were there."

After Shlomo, Rutie called. "You said that you had a lot to do today and I came early and you weren't home."

"So, why did you not come at 8 o'clock like I told you? I called you last night to come at 8 o'clock. You did not come at 8 o'clock. You did not come at eight and a quarter. At 8:30 I went by myself."

"I was there at 8:30."

"No, you were not. I left at 8:30."

Rutie said nothing but Irene knew what she was thinking.

91 YEARS OLD! She has a weak heart and cancer. She can't hear without a hearing aid and she can't see without eyeglasses. She is thin as a matchstick and as strong as one. What does she think she is?

"I was there two minutes after 8:30."

"Come tomorrow. We have to go to the store. The children are coming for Shabbat."

"Maybe two minutes after 8:30. No more than five."

"Tomorrow. The children are coming and I have to cook."

Then Yitzhak, her brother, called.

"Where were you'?

"First I went to the heart doctor. Rutie did not come so I took a bus. Rutie is afraid of terrorists and goes only by taxi. I do not like to pay for taxis all of the time. Then I went to have my hearing aid fixed. Then I went to the shoe store. I need new shoes. After that, I went to the *shuk*. Rutie is afraid to go to the shuk. Too many bombs. She goes only to the supermarket. I bought what I could carry and then I came home"

"You are crazy! You're too old to go by yourself. What do you have a helper for? What could have happened if you fell? You could have killed yourself. Are you stupid?"

Irene sighed. *What else would I expect from my baby brother? He is my only brother and I am his only sister.*

Then Miriam, Irene's sister-in-law, called.

"Where were you?"

Irene was losing her patience.

"Where could I have been? I was not home."

Miriam laughed.

"I am so relieved that you are all right."

Just as Irene put the telephone in its cradle, the doorbell rang. It was her granddaughter, Shula.

"Savta! Savta!" Shula was breathless as if she had been running, as indeed, she had been. "I tried to call you all morning. Where were you?"

"I am so sorry. I am so very sorry that I left the house." Irene was almost serious.

"I have something to tell you. I found a job and I start tomorrow. Would it be all right for me to stay here with you until I find a place to live? It is too far for me to come every day from the kibbutz."

Irene walked over to embrace Shula but Shula, moving more quickly, hugged Irene, enveloping her so that just the top of Irene's head peeped out. They exchanged a dozen kisses. Irene's eyes sparkled and Shula's face glowed with joy.

"There is much to do now and I will have to go out now but I will be back soon."

Shula left so quickly that she left Irene standing in the middle of the room with her arms still outstretched.

When Irene put her arms down, she realized that she had not eaten since breakfast.

I will eat a piece of pita, fresh and warm from the shuk, with humus and a cup of coffee and then sit in front of the television until Shula returns.

Just as Irene had taken her first bite, the doorbell rang. The insistent ringing alerted Irene. *Somehow,* she thought, *that did not sound like Shula's ring.* Irene looked through the peephole set in the door.

A strange man with a heavy black and gray beard, dressed in a black hat and coat, stood in obvious distress. Long curls on each side of his head revealed a hassidic Jew, a stranger in the neighborhood.

"What do you want?" she asked without opening the door.

"Please, I have to go to the toilet, I am sorry but nobody else in the building is home."

Irene decided to let him in. She pointed the way and he followed quickly.

Now what do I do? What if he's an Arab dressed like a Jew? There was just an Arab dressed as a hassidic Jew who blew up a bus with women and children. Maybe he's a murderer. What do I do?

Irene went into her kitchen. *What if he comes out of the bathroom with a gun or a knife?*

Irene saw a stick lying beside the washing machine. She picked it up, held it as high over her head as she could and stood by the bathroom door.

When the stranger came out, he was startled to see Irene wielding a stick and looking as mean and menacing as a little 91 year old woman could look.

"What, what's this?" he stuttered.

Irene explained.

"Please, call me Mr. Gross. I am a real Jew and I will not hurt you. Please put away your stick before you hurt yourself."

The doorbell rang. Irene, stick in hand, let Shula in. Shula, startled at the sight of Irene's stick and at the sight of a strange man in her grandmother's home, opened her eyes and mouth wide to scream.

Mr. Gross smiled and, his bright brown eyes twinkling, turned to Irene.

"You are a very kind and brave woman. Thank you very much."

He left and Irene explained to Shula. She laughed.

"Why are you laughing?

Shula looked long and lovingly into her grandmother's weakened eyes.

"Savta, you are the most amazing person I know. Only if I am lucky, very lucky, will I learn to be just like you."

Secrets

"I am ready to meet my Maker." Irene spoke softly, earnestly, each word measured. She meant what she said.

"I could not breathe this morning. I wanted to bake a cake but instead I sat down and did nothing. Now I feel better."

What Irene did not say was that the pacemaker test results were not good. Her pacemaker was all right. Her heart was not.

Katya, Irene's daughter had just arrived, and still taking off her coat, thought for a moment before she answered. She knew Irene's heart was weak and becoming weaker. Irene's doctor had called her.

"Now that you are ninety-two years old, you are ready? When you were ninety-one you weren't ready? What makes you so sure your Maker is ready to meet you? Maybe He has enough problems. Besides, we need you here. Not only that, you need a new coat."

Irene laughed. "What do I need a new coat for? I would have to break it in. I have a coat and it is already broken in."

"You broke this coat in seventeen years ago. Now it is broken up. Later, we will go shopping."

Irene was about to say something but was interrupted by the doorbell. Katya opened the door and was greeted by a huge bouquet of flowers followed by Avi, Katya's son, and Edna, her daughter-in-law.

"What's this? Flowers? Why flowers? It's not my birthday." Irene rose from her chair, smiling broadly. "You are here in the middle of the day? This is a big surprise."

Avi did not expect to see his mother there. "You told her!" Avi spoke without thinking. "I knew you would. I should have said nothing. I should have known that you couldn't keep a secret."

"Since when couldn't I keep a secret?" Katya was indignant. "How many secrets did you tell me that I didn't keep? And look who's talking? Since when could you keep a secret? Nobody could tell you anything without finding it all over the neighborhood and in the newspapers the next day."

"Secrets? What secrets? What are you talking about?" Irene could also be indignant. "Why is nobody talking to me? And what are the flowers for? It's not my birthday. It's not even before Shabbat. It's only an ordinary day."

Belying her words, a twinkle in Irene's eyes and a broad smile brightened her face. Looking from one to the other she understood why Avi and Edna had brought flowers and she was going to make the most of the moment.

Edna blushed. "The flowers are for you. You are going to be a great-grandmother in six months."

Avi, standing tall and proud, spoke in a loud, clear voice. "Savta, Mazel Tov! Congratulations! We are pregnant! The doctor said today that it's official." He, too, was making the most of the moment.

Irene had been waiting for this for a long time. Avi and Edna had been married for eight years.

Everyone kissed and hugged, shedding tears of happiness.

"I have cake in the freezer. We will have coffee or tea and a glass of milk for Edna." Irene hardly needed to say anything. She always had cake in the freezer and something in the refrigerator to go with it.

When Katya went into the kitchen to help, Irene turned on her.

"You knew and didn't tell me? You could have said something."

"Avi wanted to surprise you. You heard him. If I would've told you, you wouldn't have had such a nice surprise and Avi and Edna would have been disappointed. So, what's so terrible? And you're going to tell me that you have no secrets?" Katya smiled mischievously.

"No. I have no secrets." Irene lied.

"What is important is if you are happy. Are you happy?"

"Yes, very happy."

"This afternoon we will shop for a new coat for you and we will look for some things for the baby if we have time." Katya left no room for discussion.

Irene did not argue.

They did not go shopping for a new coat that afternoon. When they were about to start out Irene, again, had difficulty breathing. Katya took her to the hospital, instead.

AMERICA

America I

To my dearest granddaughter, Elise,

I remember being 10 years old, going on 11, and being in the fifth grade as you are now. I remember becoming more aware of the world and being both curious and afraid to know what my place would be in it. I remember the fifth grade, in particular, because I was learning to prepare for the future.

My mother always envied me my going to school. She would have been happy to go but was not allowed. In the Polish *shtetl* or town, where Mama was born and grew up, only boys, like Mama's two brothers, were educated to read and write in Yiddish and Hebrew. Girls who came from well-off families were also educated but my mother's family was poor. Neither Mama nor her three sisters ever went to school in Poland. They grew up not knowing how to read or write.

"What do you need birthday presents for?" Mama asked me when I was in first grade. Everybody else in my class had birthday presents on his birthday. When it was my birthday, they all wanted me to tell them about my presents. I went home and told Mama and she said to me, "You have the best present of all. You're learning to read and write!"

So, that is what I said the next day when I went back to school. Proudly, I looked my classmates in their eyes and said, "I don't need any presents. I'm getting an American education!" Their peals of laughter bothered me for a long time.

Only later in life did I learn that, except for Mama and me, nobody would have chosen to go to school. It was the law.

Mama did learn to read and write. But she had to teach herself and then only when her children were almost grown and she had the leisure to do so. When my cousin Milly became a third grade teacher she gave Mama the third grade reader and workbook her class was using. Mama read the reader and worked through the workbook, one page at a time, every evening, until she had read every page and completed every assignment. After that, she could read other things as well. In time, Mama learned to read even difficult and complicated things.

My mother would have been your great-grandmother. Had she lived to this time, she would have been about one hundred years old. She would have loved you as I do.

Mama liked to talk about her coming to America. In Mama's shtetl, America was called the land where gold and silver lined the streets. Anybody who worked hard, they said, could become rich. To my mother, America was better than a land of gold and silver. To Mama, America was a land where there was always something to eat and no one ever had to go hungry. That was because Mama and her parents and her five brothers and sisters were always hungry in Poland. Her father, my *Zayde* or grandfather, worked day and night when there was work for him to do and still there was not enough to eat. That was when my Zayde, with my *Babbe*, my mother's mother, decided to sell whatever they could to buy a ship's passage to America. Because there was only enough money to buy passage for Zayde, it was decided that as soon as he had saved enough money in America, he would bring all of his family across the ocean to be with him.

Zayde worked hard and, in good time, earned enough money to bring his family to America. But, as bad luck would have it, World War I broke out and it was too dangerous for passenger ships to cross the ocean. Those were years of utter misery for Mama and her family. Even when my Uncle Meyer, Mama's oldest brother, became a bakers' apprentice and was able to bring a few coins home to spend and bread to eat, it was not nearly enough. Even going to the potato fields and gleaning the potatoes which were left after the harvest and selling them was not enough. Mama told me that my Aunt Rose, Mama's youngest sister, was three years old when she learned to walk because she was not strong enough until then.

"The Polish tax collectors, made our lives even more miserable," Mama told me. Having nothing to give them and seeing that there was nothing to take, they playfully punched each other and roared with laughter at the joke they were about to play. They took the quilts, which were Babbe and Zayde's wedding presents, stripping the beds bare.

As soon as Mama was old enough to carry a child around in her arms—I suppose, Elise, that she must have started when she was younger than you—she had to go to work. And that's what Mama's job was, to carry a baby around all day long. At that time and in that place, even for the well-off family that Mama worked for, there were no diapers, baby carriages, high-chairs or playpens. Mama had a couple of rags on her arm and carried their newest baby around all day long. She was responsible for cleaning up all of the baby's messes, as well.

For this, Mama was paid with something to eat, hardly more than a crust of bread and a glass of milk. Mama had asked whether she could have something on her bread, like, perhaps, olive oil from the jar standing in the kitchen. She was not allowed. Well, she was not allowed, that is, except on the day when a rat was discovered drowned in the olive oil jar. On that day, Mama was told, she was could have as much olive oil as she wanted.

Mama told me that she said, "No." but that she said it very politely.

Finally, finally, the war was over and the ship's tickets arrived. My mother, and her mother and her five brothers and sisters went to America. Her father, my Zayde, with his black hat and beard and waistcoat flying in the wind, met his family at the pier and took them to his home, a room behind a rabbi's house near Delancey Street on the Lower East Side of Manhattan.

At that time and to that area, came all of the Yiddish-speaking immigrants from Eastern Europe after they left their ships and set foot on dry land. There, like Mama and her family, everybody spoke Yiddish. It was the only language that everybody understood.

After the welcome, there was a deep silence. That was when Babbe nudged Zayde, and told him as gently as she could, that his family was hungry.

"Of course, of course!" Zayde exclaimed happily and left to bring something to eat. He went to the nearest bakery and brought back two huge, freshly baked *challah*s which he proudly presented to his wife. The first thing Babbe did was to put one challah aside. More important to Babbe than having something to eat right away was to make sure that there would be something left to eat later. Then Babbe started to tear off pieces of the other to give to everybody.

"Nay, Mama!" declared Zayde, taking out the other challah as well. "This is America! Nobody goes hungry in America. In America, we can eat both challahs at once. When we are hungry, I will buy more."

"Do you understand why we felt that we were in a truly wonderful country?" Mama asked me many years later. "In America, we could eat two challahs at once."

"Tatte," my mother asked her father after she had eaten as much challah as she could. "Where do I find a job?"

"In America, everything is easy, Beila, my daughter. You buy a newspaper, you ride on the trolley car, and, then, you find a job."

And that's what Mama did. The very next morning Mama found a newspaper stand, bought a newspaper, climbed onto a trolley car, sat down, and waited patiently. Some people left, others climbed aboard, more people left and, finally, the trolley stopped and didn't move. Only Mama sat and waited.

"This is the last stop." The Yiddish-speaking conductor looked at Mama curiously. "Where do you want to go?"

"I'm looking for a job."

"Looking for a job?' The conductor was puzzled.

"I asked my father how to find a job and this is what he said, 'Buy a newspaper, take a ride on a trolley car and then you'll find a job.' So, here is the newspaper and here I am sitting on the trolley car. So, where's the job?"

"So?" I asked Mama. "Then what happened?"

"The conductor took me back to my father." Mama laughed. "I found a job soon enough."

My Mama, your father's Babbe, was, at that time, 15 years old.

Elise, my eldest, darling granddaughter, there are other stories to tell. There are stories about my father, and stories about how my mother and father met, fell in love, and married and stories about how it was when we were children. I will tell them one at a time.

Love and kisses,
Savta

America II

My dearest darling Elise,

You made me very happy when you told me that you enjoyed reading the letter to you about Mama, my mother. Now I will tell you about Papa, my father, who would have been your great-grandfather and was your Daddy's Zayde.

Papa, Aaron Shear, was born in 1899 and grew up in Russia in a *shtetl*, or Jewish town, called Krasilov. His family's trade was rope-making from which they made a living. "Before Passover, when we were children," he told me, "we were told that if we were good and behaved ourselves, we could each have a whole egg at Seder. If we were bad, only half an egg." You see, Elise, the Shear family could afford enough eggs for all of the children, which meant something in those days.

"One time," Papa said, "Russian soldiers were stationed in our home." At that time and in that place, Elise, people were not asked whether or not they wanted to provide bed and board for soldiers passing through their town. The townspeople, like Papa's mother and father, were ordered to do so and they dared not disobey. These soldiers happened to stay over on Shabbat and were so impressed by Papa's Mama lighting the Shabbat candles and making the blessing over them (just as we do today, Elise) that they went out the next day and returned with as many Shabbat candles as they could find. They gave them all to Papa's Mama.

Papa's grandfather lived to be 102 years old but Papa's father, Motte-Fishel Shear, for whom your great-uncle Murray was named, died suddenly at a much younger age. He did not live to see his children grow into fine adults and marry and have children of their own.

His death was a terrible shock to the entire family. The day that Papa's father died terrible cries rent the sky and rose up past the clouds to the heavens above Krasilov.

In the midst of this great anguish my father's grandfather sat himself down at the table and shouted, "I'm hungry! I want to eat!"

The wailing stopped immediately and jaws, wet from tears, were frozen silent.

"How can you think of food at a time like this?" Papa's Mama asked Papa's grandfather. "Do you not understand what a terrible calamity we have here today? How can you think of food?"

"He is dead!" Papa's grandfather said. "There is nothing more to be done for him. I am alive and I am hungry and I want to eat!"

Papa, like Mama, liked to talk to us, when we were children, about how he came to America. Do you remember, Elise, my telling you about the terrible time Mama and her family suffered through in Poland during World War I? Around the same time, around 1918-1919, Russia was torn apart by a bloody civil war called the Russian Revolution. Armies marched through towns gathering all of the boys and men they could find and forced them to join their ranks.

Soldiers came to Papa's home and Papa was one of the unlucky boys they found. He was marched off to be a soldier in an army he cared nothing about. *Now, what am I going to do?* He asked himself. He thought about what he was going to do all that day and all through the night.

The next morning when Papa opened his eyes, he also opened his mouth wide as it could go and screamed a blood-curdling scream at the top of his lungs. He tried to stand up but immediately doubled over in pain. "I'm sick! I'm sick!" he shouted. "I'm D-Y-I-N-G!" He stood up and screamed again.

The commanding officer came over and sent him to the doctor immediately. Papa walked to the building which housed the doctor's office, walked through the front door and then kept walking until he reached the back door. Out he went as fast as he could go. On his way out of the camp, Papa met up with a *landsman,* neighbor, who happened to be driving home in a horse-drawn cart. He hid Papa under a heavy robe and straw in the back of the cart and they both arrived home safely.

For the rest of the war, Papa hid in a hayloft. Once, when other soldiers came looking for recruits for *their* army, they not only searched the house, they searched the barn as well. They unsheathed their bayonets and poked the hay every which way with their long, bare knives. Fortunately, they missed Papa and he escaped unhurt.

"But I had such a terrible scare." He told us many years later. "When I had climbed up into the hayloft before the soldiers came my hair was brown. After they had left and I climbed down, everybody could see that it had turned completely white."

Papa's hair stayed white. When Mama and he were married, they had wedding photos taken. In all of the photos stood a proud and handsome man with a full head of completely white hair.

After the war was over and my Papa no longer had to hide, his Mama decided that he should go to America. My Papa's older brother, Uncle Morris, was already there so he would not be alone. The decision to send Papa to America came, however, in 1922 just after the United States government had passed immigration laws. Now, instead of just paying for passage, like my Mama's family did, people, like Papa, who wanted to go to America had to apply to the American government first. You see, Elise, a quota system had been established and few people from Russia were going to be allowed to enter each year. Papa would have had to wait years if he would have applied to enter the United States under the quota system. Only after he would have received permission to enter could Papa book passage on a ship knowing that he would not be turned back when he arrived.

So, what was Papa to do? It was decided that he book passage on a ship going to Cuba which is very close to the United States. Cuba had no immigration laws and Papa would have no problem being accepted there.

In Cuba, Papa found himself a job as an assistant to a kosher butcher and earned enough money to support himself and to save a little as well. After living in Cuba for 1½ years, Papa arranged to be smuggled into America on a ship bringing bananas to the U.S. Before ships left port, immigration and customs officials would board and check the passengers and cargo to make sure that everything and everybody was there according to law. But before the inspectors climbed aboard this ship, Papa was placed inside the large walk-in refrigerator, where the inspectors would not think to look. He stayed there until they left and the ship set sail. After Papa left the refrigerator, he was treated like any other passenger. However, as soon as the ship approached Florida, he had to return to the refrigerator until it was safe for him to leave.

Then, with his brother's address in his pocket and little else besides, Papa had the good fortune to meet up with Yiddish-speaking strangers who were able to guide him along the way. Papa made his way by train from the southern tip of Florida to New York City where, again, he had the good fortune to find strangers who guided him to the door of his brother, Morris, where he and his bride, Fanny, lived.

Papa and then, later, Mama were never to forget that Papa was an illegal alien. They lived with the fear that he would be found out and sent back to Russia. When I was a little girl I was told that should a stranger ask me questions about my father, I was to say nothing but come home right away and tell Mama. Papa was afraid to apply for citizenship for fear of being sent back to Russia.

Papa did become a U.S. citizen many years later. When one of my older brothers, your great-uncle Irv, was ready to graduate from college, he decided that it was time for Papa to apply to become a citizen. Irv took it upon himself to fill out the application for Papa. Usually, an applicant must wait five years in order to be invited to go to court and take tests to become a citizen. Papa, however, received a notice to appear in court right away. Mama, my mother's youngest sister, Aunt Rosie, and, of course, Irv, went along to serve as character witnesses and, also, to give Papa moral support.

They were all very nervous when they left for the courthouse. *What if it was possible to deport Papa after all those years*, they asked themselves. I did my share and stayed behind and babysat for my cousins, Ned and Arthur, Aunt Rosie's children.

They returned in a much better mood. Papa had taken the oath and had become America's newest citizen.

When it had been Papa's turn to appear before the judge, he had trembled. Questions like, "What is your name?" and "Where do you live?" were no problem. But when he was asked THE question: "When did you arrive in America?" Papa turned pale as a ghost and shrugged. He could not remember. The judge then picked up a file from his desk and told Papa that, according to his records, he had arrived in 1924 on a banana boat that had come to the U.S. from Cuba. Papa and everybody with him were dumbfounded.

The judge then handed Papa a pencil and paper and asked him to write, "I am here." Papa shook from sheer terror. Despite the lovely spring weather, Papa was bathed in perspiration as he wrote a small case "i" in a very shaky hand. Hesitatingly, he put a dot above it and then, shaking even more, could not continue. Papa had never learned to read or write in English.

The judge looked at Papa, Mama, Aunt Rose and Irv and then looked at his watch.

"Jack," he called over to another judge. "How about breaking for lunch?"

Then he asked Papa to raise his right hand and Papa was sworn in as a citizen.

That is how Papa became an American citizen and never again had to worry about being sent back to Russia.

Elise, I hope that you like this letter, also. There are other stories to tell but it will take time.

Love and kisses,
Savta

America III

To my darling granddaughter, Elise,

My first two letters were about my Mama, Bella Dorsch, and my Papa, Aaron Shear, their childhoods in Poland and Russia and how each of them came to America. This letter is about how Aunt Bertha and Uncle Nathan and Mama and Papa met, fell in love, and were married.

Mama's parents, Babbe and Zayde, lived, at first, with their six children in a tiny apartment on the Lower East Side of Manhattan in New York City. How did eight people manage to live together in a small apartment, you ask? Where did everybody sleep, for instance?

No matter how tiny, the apartment was large enough to accommodate three double beds. For Babbe and Zayde, a double bed presented no problems. It was roomy enough for two. Mama's brothers, my Uncles Meyer and Irving, shared the second bed and they also had no problem.

Mama and her three sisters, however, had a problem. Four young ladies, however thin and agreeable, did not fit easily in a bed meant for two. They quarreled all of the time. During the cold, damp winters, each wanted to sleep on the inside where it was warmer. During the hot, humid summers, everyone wanted to sleep on the outside.

My Aunt Bertha, Mama's oldest sister, was the first in the family to marry. Almost from the time Nathan Solomon and she were introduced to each other, they knew that they wanted to spend the rest of their lives together. Proudly, Bertha brought Nathan home to meet the family.

Zayde, upon meeting Nathan, however, was not pleased. Nathan, you see, was born and raised in Syria where Jews did not speak Yiddish and followed different customs and traditions. Nathan had learned to speak Yiddish only after he had come to America.

As far as Zayde was concerned, the only REAL Jews came from Poland. Nathan did not even look like a Jew to Zayde. Instead of being tall and fair skinned, Nathan was short in stature and swarthy. As far as Zayde was concerned, only REAL Jews were acceptable as son-in-laws. Nathan was unacceptable.

Despite all reasoning, Bertha stood firm. She knew who she wanted and she was going to marry Nathan.

In desperation, Uncle Meyer decided to take matters into his own hands to solve the problem. He gathered several of his burly friends together and they lay in wait for Nathan as he approached the house. Then they jumped him, beat him, and left him bruised and bleeding from head to toe. Shocked, Nathan could not even defend himself.

"Let that be a lesson to you." Meyer told him as he gave him a last kick. "Stay away from my sister."

He never expected to see Nathan again.

He was mistaken. As soon as Nathan recovered, he came to the house. But this time he did not come to see Bertha but to see Zayde. He asked Zayde to go with him to visit HIS rabbi.

There Nathan demonstrated that he was learned in Jewish studies, customs and traditions and was, indeed, as REAL a Jew as Zayde, himself.

They returned home together where Bertha was waiting for them, unsmiling, arms folded over her chest, and ready to defy the world. It was not necessary.

Before she could say a word, Zayde told her, "It's all right, Bertha. You want to marry Nathan? Go, marry him! He is not only a Jew; he is also a *mensch*, a brave and good man." Bertha unfolded her arms, wrapped them around Zayde and gave him a hug and kiss.

Then she went over to Nathan.

Everybody danced with joy at Bertha and Nathan's wedding and wished the young couple much joy and happiness. The three remaining sisters were especially joyous. From that night on, there would be more room in bed.

Mama was the next sister to marry. At that time, most new immigrants in New York worked in the garment industry. Mass produced, ready-made clothing was sent from there to all over the United States. Both Mama and Papa worked in the garment industry and this had a lot to do with how they met.

Actually, Mama had met another young man, who also worked in the garment industry, named Moishe, before she met Papa. They liked each other a lot and Mama brought him home to meet Zayde and the rest of her family.

Again, Zayde was not thrilled. Moishe, you see, was what was called in those days a 'free-thinker.' Free-thinkers were people who were open to new ideas and new philosophies. Since people cannot be both open to new ideas and faithful to old ones at the same time, traditions, the religious traditions especially, were often abandoned. Moishe was no exception. So, one day, when Moishe came to the house to call on Mama, Zayde called him aside.

"Young man, you see that my daughter, Bella, comes from a traditional kosher home. When she marries, she is going to keep a kosher home just like her mother."

"Kosher, shmosher," Moishe answered with a shrug. "When the dishes are washed, they're clean. What's kosher, shmosher?"

"Young man, young man," Zayde replied, barely containing his anger, "You are not for my daughter and my daughter is not for you. Go home!"

Moishe left but Mama was not happy.

Zayde then decided that he, himself, would find a suitable husband for Mama. He arranged for Mama to meet his friends' sons. He also went to a *shadchen,* a matchmaker, and saw that she was introduced only to pious yeshiva students.

After every date, Zayde asked her, "Nu, so?"

Mama answered, "I'm sorry, *Tatte*, but he didn't like me."

Actually, Mama told me that she didn't like THEM but she was afraid that if she told her father the truth, he would have been angry with her. This way, there was nothing Zayde could say.

Ironically, Moishe was the unintentional matchmaker who introduced Papa to Mama. One hot, summer Sunday, Mama, her sisters, and her friends took the subway from Manhattan and went to the beach in Coney Island. They went to cool off with a swim in the ocean and to relax on a blanket spread over the golden sand. While they were spreading their blankets and arranging their things, Mama looked up to see Moishe in the water with a tall, handsome stranger. Mama watched them for a little while and then she had to laugh. While Moishe was swimming, the stranger, who turned out to be Papa, jumped up and down, splashing himself as old women often do. He did not know how to swim. It was at that moment that Mama fell in love.

Papa, then recently arrived in America, was Moishe's new apprentice. It was natural for Moishe to show Papa what America was like and to take him to the beach to enjoy a nice, summer day. He introduced Papa and Mama to each other and Papa also fell in love.

Actually, Papa was not much more observant than Moishe but succeeded in hiding this from Zayde. Papa refused o make an issue of his religious observances. At that time, Papa lived a distance from Mama on the other side of a long bridge. Ordinarily, he took the streetcar and came and left whenever he pleased. On Shabbat, however, riding on streetcars was forbidden. Nevertheless, Papa visited on Shabbat.

"The weather was good so I walked over the bridge," he would say.

He said the same thing even on days when the weather was cold and stormy. Zayde looked at Papa without expression and said nothing. Mama turned her head to hide her smile.

By this time, Zayde had learned not to ask too many questions. He had learned to not expect perfection, not in himself, not in his family, and, certainly, not in his sons-in-law. So, everybody was happy, more or less.

When Mama and Papa were married, there was great rejoicing in the Dorsch household. Mama's sisters, my Aunt Anna and my Aunt Rosie, had the entire double bed to themselves.

Love and kisses,
Savta

Making a Living

Just because Mom and Pop chose each other to love and marry and just because their wedding in the mid-1920s was a joyous occasion did not mean that, just like in the movies, they walked into the sunset holding hands and lived happily ever after.

When my brother, Murray, was born just a year later, everything was right with their world. Not only did they have a healthy baby but he was a boy! Boys were considered true blessings. Girls less so. When their second child, my brother, Irv, was born eighteen months later, their family was complete. Other children would be superfluous.

At that time, too many girls born in succession without a boy to break the monotony could end in divorce. My mother's brother, Uncle Meyer, refused to visit his wife, Aunt Dora, in the hospital when she gave birth to their second child, another girl. *It was her fault,* Uncle Meyer thought. *She was the one who gave birth, wasn't she?* Redemption for Aunt Dora came when the next two children were boys.

Mom quit work as soon as she became noticeably pregnant but that was all right. Pop, after all, was earning a man's salary.

Unfortunately, the Great Depression intervened and Pop no longer earned a man's salary. There was no work. There was no money. Not in the garment industry. Not anywhere.

At best, work in the garment industry had been seasonal and the busiest season, which was for winter clothing, ended just before Passover.

Like a true bride-to-be, Mom had asked Pop how much money he earned.

"Two hundred dollars a week," was the proud answer.

At that time, two hundred dollars a week was a LOT of money. A family could eat well on five dollars a week.

Mom had laughed. She knew what Pop had meant. Pop earned two hundred dollars a week for the two weeks ending before Passover. For the rest of the year contracts were few and far between and there was little more to be earned. The two hundred dollars a week for two weeks every year was their basis for middle class survival.

The Great Depression, when it arrived in 1929, made life more complicated. Occasionally a salesman would receive an order. He would rent a loft, set up shop and hire workers. They would bring their own equipment.

Pop would lug a heavy iron with him to work. When the order was filled, the workers would be paid and the shop would be dissolved. Then they would wait for the next order.

Sometimes the order would be finished and the workers would not be paid. They would go to work and find the shop's door padlocked. Their boss had disappeared with their money.

People found different ways to survive. Pop played pinochle. When he won, they paid the rent on time. When he didn't, he hoped to win next time.

The problem, actually, wasn't Pop's, it was Mom's. It was up to her to make do with what there was or wasn't. That was when Mom became an independent businesswoman.

Uncle Nathan, Mom's brother-in-law, made raisin brandy, called Arak. Colorless, it was nevertheless, POTENT! Mom sold one full shot glass at a time to anyone who came to the door. Sometimes a couple of shot glasses were more than a customer could handle.

Murray remembered coming home from school and finding a stranger or two "sleeping it off" in front of the door. Occasionally, the stranger would puke before stretching out on the floor.

This was Mom's (and Pop's) way of "making do."

They were "making do" when I was born. Having another baby was not exactly on their agenda. Mom and Pop had lost a child not long before.

"She had a respiratory disease. Today we could cure it." Dr. Mausner, our family doctor, said casually during an office visit.

Mom had taken her sick little daughter from one hospital to another. Each hospital could do nothing but send her elsewhere. Mom took her baby in a taxi from one place to another until she died.

Mom's next pregnancy, me, was greeted with a decided lack of joy. Having two healthy sons, a lingering sorrow, and no money, Mom considered an abortion. Why she decided not to go through with it, I don't know. But, anyway, I arrived.

I was born at home. For some years, my brothers were convinced that the doctor had brought me in his satchel. Their neighbor, Mrs. Cohen's son, was an intern at the time and charged less for the delivery than the hospital would have. Another girl cheered no one.

Soon after I was born, the Great Depression began to fade and slowly, slowly, the economy improved. There were more orders for ladies' coats and suits, more work for Pop, and more money coming into the house. Were it not for a small incident, just a small incident, lasting no more than a minute or two, all would have been well. But, just for a small incident, our lives were changed.

Mom was taking me out in the baby carriage for a walk to the park when two men walking towards her from the opposite direction stopped her to ask a question.

"Where can we go to buy a number?"

The Numbers Racket was illegal gambling. Mom hardly paid attention to the two men or to what she was doing. Everybody in the neighborhood knew that the dry cleaning store owner across the street also ran a Numbers Racket on the side. Mom raised her arm and pointed.

"Don't point!" One of them said sharply. "Keep your arm down! Just tell us."

Mom told them and went right home. The next day she heard that the owner of the dry cleaning store was arrested and put in jail.

When he came out, he was furious.

"Who put the finger on me?" he roared, his face turning red-purple. "I'm going to get the one who put the finger on me." He spoke slowly and deliberately. Everyone shuddered. They all understood what he meant.

That's when Mom decided that it was time to move. With a little money put aside from her bootlegging, she bought a candy store. Then she told Pop.

"Mrs. Levy's son said that from this we could make a living. We're moving tomorrow."

Pop said nothing. He had nothing to do with selling Uncle Nathan's Arak and he wanted nothing to do with the candy store. The problem was that he had no choice. If we were moving, so was he.

What Mrs. Levy's son didn't tell Mom and what she didn't see for herself was that there were two other candy stores in the neighborhood, one across the street and another on the next street. One store could make a living for a family. Two were more difficult. Three could not. But luck was on Mom and Pop's side. Right after they took over, the other two went out of business.

Running a candy store was hard work. The store was open twenty hours a day, seven days a week and run, basically, by Mom and Pop. When my brothers grew older, they would help.

The store was closed for weddings and for the holidays of Passover, Rosh Hashanah and Yom Kippur. There were no other reasons. Illness was no excuse. The store would remain open anyway.

Mom and Pop did okay financially. When the Second World War was over, Pop went back to work in the garment industry. Mom and Pop had earned enough money to keep themselves away from hardship for the rest of their lives.

Memories—The Candy Store

The candy store that Mom and Pop owned before and during the Second World War was hardly impressive—no more than a "hole in the wall." Its width was that of a medium sized front window and adjacent front door. The length of the store was enough to contain magazines, newspapers, cigarettes, ice cream, soda, and, of course, candy.

The wall beside the door held a magazine rack filled with comic books and magazines. Meant for the illiterate or barely literate, the combination of few words and many pictures made comic books very popular.

The store would receive a fresh selection of comic books and magazines every month. My older brother, Murray would replace the leftovers with the new ones. When he finished, he would collect one of each of the new ones and bring it home. We had all of them to read at our leisure.

Nurtured by comic books, I learned to read. "Archie", "Blondie", and "Casper the Ghost" were some of the funny ones. "Superman," "Captain Marvel," and "Batman" were adventure stories. Whatever the comic, one could be sure that good sense and justice always won and that there were only happy endings.

When we finished reading the comic books, sometimes two or three times, they were collected, brought downstairs and placed back on the rack. Sometimes a customer would complain that a comic book would look worn as if it were secondhand. In that case, we would just shrug and turn our heads. A customer was entitled to his opinion.

Under the comic book and magazine rack stood piles of newspapers. When the newspapers were delivered each morning before dawn, Pop would be at the door of the candy store ready to receive them. If he wouldn't be there, they would have disappeared. Pop was at the store door just four hours after Mom and he had closed for the previous day and counted the day's receipts. He left Mom and the rest of us sleeping in the early hours to cross the street and open up.

The newspapers were collected and stacked in their proper places. The store opened and Pop was ready for business.

Around lunchtime, Mom would come down, take her place behind the counter and Pop would go upstairs. He would find a hot meal waiting for him at the table. Having eaten, he would take off his shoes, place his head on his pillow and enjoy dreamless oblivion. When he woke, Pop would then relieve Mom so that she could shop and cook dinner. That done, Mom would join Pop in the store.

The store would be busiest when school let out and when people would stop by on their way home from work. That's when my brothers and I would help.

The Sunday paper with its full section of comics was the newspaper most in demand. A regular customer could have his paper reserved so that he could sleep just a little bit longer without worrying that there would be no paper by the time he came downstairs. If he were affluent, he could have the Sunday paper delivered to his door by either Murray or Irv for the price of the newspaper plus a tip. That worked well for both my brothers until the war years when the neighborhood changed.

When we first moved into the Harlem section of Manhattan during the late 1930s, the neighborhood consisted of largely poor Irish Catholic families. As the Great Depression faded and the likelihood of war became real, the neighborhood changed. Government contracts became common and money was to be made with steady jobs. Families moved to better neighborhoods and single people from the deep South arrived. Apartments were shared by as many as ten people with not enough beds for all. Because plants with government contracts were in production twenty-four hours a day, people worked in eight hour shifts. As soon as some of the people left for work others returned and went to sleep in still warm, disheveled beds. For the most part, these people were rough and often violent.

The last time the Sunday paper was delivered to the door was when Irv rang the bell and was greeted with a drawn knife instead of coins in the palm of a hand. After that, all newspapers had to be picked up and paid for at the store.

Just past the newspapers stood an enclosed booth which contained a public telephone. Inside the booth opposite the telephone was a shelf that could serve as an uncomfortable seat for the caller. This telephone served not only those who came to the store but the entire neighborhood as well. It was used to call the doctor or the police or to inform family members of important events. It was through this telephone that Mom learned that her father had died and Pop learned that his brother had died. It was to this telephone that a neighbor could be called dripping wet from his bath, dressed in whatever hid his essentials, to answer the call. Before the war either of my brothers would be sent to fetch a neighbor and usually given a penny or two for his trouble. Or, if necessary, if either of my parents was alone in the store and no one else was available, the door would be locked and he/she would do the fetching.

The telephone booth would serve another purpose as well. I remember Mom being ill with a temperature sitting inside the booth leaning her head against the telephone and resting a little.

Between the two walls of the candy store stood a counter with stools on which a customer or two could sit. On the other side of the counter was a refrigerator box holding tubs of vanilla, chocolate, and strawberry ice cream. Against the wall behind the counter was a shelf for ice cream cones and paper containers for ice cream 'to go'. Bringing ice cream home on a sweltering day before it turned to sweet mush was a challenge.

Above the shelf were racks for cigarettes and tobacco. Cigarettes were always in demand and good money-makers even before the war. As the war years drew closer and spending money was more available, the demand for cigarettes increased. With the increase in demand came a decreasing supply. At first, Mom and Pop reserved packs of cigarettes for their favorite customers and attached surcharges for the favor.

When demand increased further, Mom and Pop became more enterprising. They would buy loose tobacco and cigarette paper and roll their own. They bought a small machine which could be filled with tobacco on top and within which a cigarette paper could be placed. A turn of the handle and one cigarette at a time would be rolled. Everyone took a turn at rolling out cigarettes. Mom and Pop not only made a lot of cigarettes, they made a lot of money despite having to charge less for the homemade variety.

Just beyond the counter lay an icebox for cold sodas. Always dependent on regular deliveries by the ice truck, large blocks of ice would be delivered. All of we smaller children would herald the arrival of the ice truck by running to the loading platform and begging for loose slivers of ice. The men would throw us whatever chips they had, sometimes grimy with dirt. The slivers would slide from our hands and fall into the street. Now what was I to do with my precious gifts?

"Kiss them and hold them up to the sky so that they could be kissed by God." My friend Patsy said.

I held the filthy things way up to the sky as high as my hands could go. Then I ate them. Whatever melted in my mouth cooled me as the best ice cream never has. The rest, well . . . , was kissed by God, wasn't it?

The block of ice delivered to the icebox had to be broken up, chipped away, by an ice pick. This was Irv's job. I would watch his hands redden and bleed from the icy water.

During the war years Coca-Cola was in short supply and, like cigarettes, also in great demand. Because Mom and Pop made a good profit on homemade cigarettes, they decided to do something about Coca-Cola. They bought jars of Coca-Cola extract and mixed their own brew in, I hate to say it, the bathtub. They refilled empty bottles and sold them as they sold regular bottles of Coke.

The problem was with the bottle cap. Originally placed on the neck of the bottle by a bottling machine, the edges were bent by the bottle opener and impossible to replace as they had been originally. The trick was to replace the cap without worrying about too many details. The bottle would lie in wait completely covered by melting ice until its time came. Then it was quickly removed, turned to the bottle opener on the wall and the cap would be popped before the customer could notice anything unusual about the cap. Per bottle, this was even more profitable. I don't remember any complaints.

Past the icebox stood a showcase full of "penny" candies. This was my domain. A child could, and often did, stand in front of the penny candy case for a half hour or more savoring the clinking sound of money in his pocket and the power of choosing.

There were thick blocks of Hooten's chocolate, sugar covered gumballs, or long strips of paper covered with rows of sugared dots. The long strips of paper had definite advantages over the other two. The paper could be torn and shared with greedy friends and/or siblings. Also, they would last a long time. Each dot had to be sucked off individually. The decision could be excruciating. Sometimes my patience ended with an unfriendly, "Nu!", and a choice was made.

The Driving License

The problem was that we had a car. It sat in front of our house for everybody to see. And admire. Mostly, to admire. Actually, the problem wasn't the car. The problem was that, except for my brother, Irv, who was in the U.S. Army during the Korean War, nobody knew how to drive. And even if one of us knew how to drive, not one of us had a license from the City of New York.

Mom and Pop bought the car for Irv. When he graduated from college he worried about being drafted into the army. Who wanted to go into the U.S. Army especially when it was fighting? It was dangerous. Besides who wanted to eat *treif,* non-kosher food? The army didn't have a kosher kitchen and the big Hebrew National kosher salami everybody took with him only went so far. And, then, where would he hide it? The other recruits hated the smell of garlic. What did they know? It's a wonder so many of them were still alive from the stuff they ate. Anyway, it was a problem.

So, when Irv found his first professional job in an airplane company on Long Island, we thought that his problems were solved. Just like that. Hooray! Everybody who had a job necessary for the war effort received a deferment. And everybody knew how important airplanes were for the war. That meant that Irv could work for as long as the deferment lasted and when the deferment was up, he could get another deferment.

Where we lived in Brooklyn we could go anywhere we wanted by New York City subway or by bus. Mostly by subway. We'd go down a long stairway, take a train, go a few stops, maybe get on another train, walk up a flight of stairs, and we'd be in any part of the city that we wanted. The trick was taking the right train to the right stop so that we wouldn't have to go to the other side of the tracks and go back again.

The city wasn't the only place we could visit. We could go anywhere in the country. If we took a train to Grand Central Station or Penn Station, we could take one of the trains from there to outside the city.

Now, here, Irv had a problem. He had to take the Long Island Railroad from Grand Central Station to go to work. Now, everybody who knew anything about the Long Island Railroad knew that it wasn't too good. It starts late and it ends up late and sometimes it would break down in the middle. Not only that but it didn't usually have heat in the winter. So, after Irv *kvetched,* moaned and groaned, a lot and then, to prove a point, had a really bad cold, Mom and Pop got together and decided to buy him a car.

Irv took lessons, studied hard, slipped the New York City driving inspector ten bucks and had a license to drive a car. Then he was a big shot! He drove it back and forth to work every day and on weekends he took us places. In between the car stood in front of the house and told the world that HERE LIVED A FAMILY WITH A CAR. Whenever we passed it in either coming or going we stopped for a second or two and paid it homage.

Then Irv's deferment was up and he couldn't get another one. The U.S. Army wanted him. Irv went to his boss who was very sorry but couldn't do anything. It was easier to hire someone to take Irv's place than to fight the U.S. government. So, Irv went into the army and the car stayed behind.

On one hand we had a car that Mom and Pop owned, free and clear, and on the other hand nobody else in the family knew how to drive. Not Mom, not Pop, not my brother, Murray, who didn't want or need one, and certainly not me. I was fifteen at the time so that it wasn't even an option.

"I'm taking driving lessons," Mom quietly announced one night while we were eating supper.

"What driving lessons?" Pop asked. "You can't read. How're you going to drive?"

Pop could not read or write either. When he came from Russia as a young man, he went to work right away. Mom, too, went to work right away after she came from Poland with her family. Neither, in the meantime, had learned to read or write English.

"What's to know about driving? I'm not blind. I can see the lights, green to go and red to stop. I can figure out what the signs say. They always have pictures on them. What's to read?"

"How are you going to get a license? It's not only driving, you have to show the City of New York that you can pass the test. How're you going to pass the reading part?"

"I have Sam, my driving teacher. Right now, he's giving me lessons every week. He said that when I'm ready to take the test he'll help me. What's the problem?"

New York City had strict rules for people who wanted a license to drive a car. The applicant was allowed to take three tests. Two failures meant that there was still a third to go but it would be the last one.

Mom failed the first two tests she took.

"I can't pass the reading part." She told me, "The inspector gives me a paper with questions and I have to check off a box with 'yes' or 'no' answer for each question. Then he takes out a watch and gives me ten minutes to finish. Sometimes I answer 'yes', other times I answer 'no' but the watch is always finished before I am. Not only I can't finish, I don't even have the right answers."

All those lessons with Sam, and Mom was nowhere. One more test to go and that was it.

When the next lesson was over, Sam sat in his seat for a minute longer than usual. Then he looked all around him to see who was there. When he didn't see anyone he knew, he took a piece of paper out of his pocket and gave it to Mom.

"It's one of the written tests the inspectors use. There are two others and they switch them around so nobody knows which one they're going to use. I couldn't get the others but I got this one. If you study it maybe it'll help. You can have it until the next test. Just don't tell anybody or I get into big trouble."

Mom didn't just study it, she practically ate it whole. Every time I came home from school, she sat me down at the kitchen table. Cookies, milk and a little conversation were one thing. This was serious stuff.

"Test me!" Mom would demand. "Go ahead, ask me the questions."

As I rattled off the questions, Mom would put an 'x' on the paper in either a 'yes' or 'no' column as if she were marking the actual paper. After a while, Mom knew all of the right answers to the questions.

Then she learned the questions by heart. All that I had to do was to start with a word and she would rattle off the rest of the question and then the right answer. Not long after that, Mom had memorized all of the questions in order or out of order. She could repeat the whole list without a mistake.

"Now I'm going to take the test." Mom told Sam.

The big day came. I came home from school and hesitated at the door. I was afraid of what I would hear. *Poor Mom! What'll she do now? What's going to happen to the car?*

I wasn't prepared for a face lit from within with joy.

"I got it! I got my license. You want to see?" Mom waved a piece of paper under my nose.

"I took the driving test and the inspector said nothing. Then he took out a paper and a watch and told me, 'Ten minutes' like always. I looked at the test and I got scared. Then I looked again. It was the same test! It was the same test Sam gave me. You should've seen how fast I finished. One, two, three! It didn't take ten minutes. It didn't even take five minutes. I filled out every question and gave it to the inspector. He put the watch away and he looked it over. 'Lady, I got to hand it to you.' he said. 'You did okay. For a lady your age you did O.K.!' Then he passed me."

Mom stood there for a moment letting it all sink in.

"Come with me. I have to buy a girdle. Then we'll go have an ice cream."

I didn't tell Mom what she already knew. The store with the girdles was only a couple of blocks away.

I just hopped into the car and off we went.

America—The Generation Gap

To say that there was a generation gap between Mom, Pop and us is not an overstatement. Mom and Pop had come from the old country after the First World War. In many ways they had brought the old country to the new country. They lived in an insulated Yiddish-speaking world of friends and relatives. Of course, they had all learned to speak English but only because of the necessity to venture forth into the strange world which was America.

That is not to say that they didn't love America. They loved it with all their hearts and souls. America was the country in which they could earn a living if they worked hard. A land where they could raise their children in peace. A land where there was no fear of religious pogroms when the citizenry went on righteous, drunken rampages to destroy, rape and murder simple people simply because they were Jews.

Also, there were no restrictions on educating their children to be good American citizens, equal to every other American citizen. Their children could have university educations if they were worthy. Their children would have choices that they themselves never dreamed of having in their youth. Nobody, especially neither my brothers nor I, could say anything against America to our parents.

They were especially proud that their children were American born and could read and write English since they never learned to read and write in any language. Actually, Pop could read and write in Yiddish and could read Hebrew, since it was necessary for his Bar Mitzvah, but he did not understand what he was reading. Mom was taught nothing in the old country. She was a girl and not worthy of an education.

To Mom and Pop, America was a miracle. To me, America was a way of life and I accepted my freedoms casually, unquestioningly, as if they were my due.

I had no fear of persecution even during the McCarthy years when I was a teenager. Senator McCarthy exemplified the hatred of Communism at a time when there was a common fear that it would replace the philosophy of the free world. It was a shameful time in America's history when anyone called a Communist could easily become a pariah of society.

Still, when I accepted a copy of The Daily Worker, given gratis, on the corner of Macy's Department Store next to the subway station, I had no fear of persecution. I knew my rights. I was just curious.

Well, anyway, I brought it home to read. But, then, I made a big mistake. I told Mom what it was that I was reading. Whew! That was when the you-know-what hit the fan.

"A COMMUNIST NEWSPAPER? YOU'RE READING A COMMUNIST NEWSPAPER? In this *goldene medine*, this wonderful country, YOU'RE READING A COMMUNIST PAPER! You were born here and have a home and something to eat. You don't know what it is to go hungry. You don't know how lucky you are to have an American education. And this is what you do? This is the way you treat America? You want to be arrested and go to jail? You want a pogram against Jews? I know what a pogrom was like. You don't . . ."

The rampage continued. I threw the paper into the trash. It wasn't enough. Mom ranted at me full speed at the top of her lungs. I removed the paper from the trash and very ostentatiously, just under her nose, tore it up into tiny shreds. Still not enough. Mom didn't stop her onslaught until the early hours of the morning.

Bleary eyed the next morning, I walked to the subway station, meeting our next door neighbor, Angie, on the way.

"What was your mother screaming at you for last night?" Angie wanted to know.

My head sank between my shoulders. "Damned if I know." I slunk by.

Macy's Department Store's corner, next to the subway station, was a good place for people to distribute all kinds of things. Much of which I found uninteresting. Then, for a while, there was a couple distributing the Christian Bible under a sign that said that it was free for Jews. I had passed the sign many times but the more I saw it the more it bothered me. I took it personally. Did they mean to challenge us?

"I am a Jew." I stated flatly one day and I put my hand out. I don't know whether I really wanted the Bible or whether I just felt like taking them up on their dare.

Open-mouthed but not saying a word, I was given a copy. I accepted.

Now what? I asked myself. *If I brought home any of the sexually explicit, commonly forbidden books for teenagers like the Kinsey Report, Studs Lonigan, or Lady Chatterley's Lover, any of the books that our generation covered in plain brown paper and read surreptitiously, there wouldn't even have been a ripple.*

Actually, Mom and Pop had known about sex for a long time already and took it a lot less seriously than our generation did.

But the Christian Bible? That's another story entirely. If The Daily Worker gave Mom heartburn, what would the Bible do?

I took the subway home and read it on the way. I wasn't impressed. The first trash bin that I saw after I alighted received it as a donation. I was definitely, very definitely, not taking any chances.

The big culture clash for Mom and Pop came a few years later after we flew the coop, so to speak. After the first shock of having all three of us married and out of the house within the space of a year, Mom and Pop also flew the coop, so to speak.

They decided to spend a carefree winter in Florida with their buddies and enjoy the freedom which they didn't seek but found to be a blessing nonetheless.

"But what about paying your income tax?" We wanted to know. "The due date for income tax is March 15th and you won't be home until April."

"Income tax, shmincome tax!" Pop retorted. "So, we don't pay for one year. They're going to care a lot? The American government is going to go bankrupt if they don't get our money? They're not going to go bankrupt." Pop answered his own question. "They have enough people to take money from. If anybody asks you, we're down in Florida enjoying the sunshine and don't know from taxes."

We were a little skeptical but what could we say? And, to tell the truth, nothing did happen, seemingly. Mom and Pop enjoyed their vacation and came back home tanned and rosy. They seemed to have proven their point.

That is, they did until they received an official letter from the Internal Revenue Service of the United States of America requesting their appearance at their office with detailed financial documentation. Maybe Mom and Pop couldn't read or write English but THAT they understood.

To say that they were nervous was an understatement. That the official who was assigned to their case spoke to them in Yiddish did nothing to set them at ease.

"You have interest from savings in the bank? You have to pay taxes on that. You have a pension? More taxes. You made a contribution to the Hebrew Home for the Aged? You didn't make a contribution. Who do you have in the home? A mother, father, uncle? It's not a contribution. You don't get a deduction."

Mom and Pop kept silent.

"And for not paying your taxes on time, you have to pay a fine yet."

Still Mom and Pop said not a word.

"And you should thank me," the tax examiner said, closing the file with a flourish. He looked into both of their eyes and smiled. "Anybody else would have made you pay double."

Pop paid.

Afterwards, when Mom and Pop told and retold their story, they made it clear to everyone who listened that they had had a lesson in American law and culture.

My Wedding Gown

"Frieda isn't lending her wedding gown to *anybody* after her wedding. Not to you. Not to anybody. I'm keeping it for a family heirloom. When it will be time for her daughters to get married and need a gown, it will be here with me." Mrs. Cohen, at that time, my future sister-in-law's mother, crossed her well-rounded arms across her ample breasts and that was that.

What kind of family heirloom? I thought. Who had family heirlooms? In our Jewish community during the 1950s, who had family heirlooms? Family, yes. Family all over the place. But heirlooms? What was left in Eastern Europe before the war stayed there. Everybody who had the good fortune to spend the war years in America did not complain. Mrs. Cohen had been watching too many movies.

"Frieda and Irv aren't even married yet and you're worrying about their daughters?"

Mrs. Cohen was unmoved.

I could have argued more. I could have said that a $60.00 dress from Klein's Department Store basement didn't make for much of an heirloom. Klein's was famous for getting rid of items that didn't sell by knocking prices down to practically nothing. Wedding gowns were no exception.

At that time *everybody* borrowed or rented wedding gowns and tuxedos. They were too expensive to buy and they were worn only once. You had to be crazy to spend money like that.

Anyway, once in a while somebody would get a bargain like Frieda did and when that happened everybody shared. If I had found a bargain gown first you could bet your life that Mrs. Cohen would have been only too happy to borrow it.

That was the year that both my brothers and I were married within a nine month period. Irv and Frieda were married in January, we were marred in June, and Murray and Sydelle in September. It was hard on our parents but that's the way it was.

Since Sydelle's father, Mr. Goldworm, was a caterer, he offered to make all of the arrangements at his hall and give us a good price. The offer was too good to refuse. We were all married in the same place.

So, the wedding gown became *the* problem. After I left Mrs. Cohen and Frieda, I went home to talk it over with Mom and Pop. After all, they were paying for everything. In those days that's what the parents of the bride did.

But we were in luck. At that time, I worked for an accounting firm. Not that I did much. I was what the boss called, "The girl." Nameless, I was one of a succession of 'girls' who was hired to answer the telephone, greet people as they arrived and make myself generally useful by filing, licking stamps, and sealing envelopes. We were hired and replaced in rapid succession because we never stayed around for very long. We always went on to bigger and better things which included getting married. The boss never bothered to learn any of our names.

Anyway, one of the firm's accounts was a bridal gown manufacturer.

"The manufacturer's policy is to make wedding gowns for their employees and their families at cost. Since you're an employee of their accounting firm the policy applies to you. I'll talk to them." Al, the accountant who handled the bridal gown manufacturer, gave me a big smile and a wink.

To Mom and Pop, when I told them, it was like music to their ears.

The day after Al told me that it was okay and that they would treat me as one of the employees, Mom and I showed up at the shop. We chose the gown from a catalog and they cut the fabric according to my measurements.

My wedding dress cost Mom and Pop $100 which wasn't a big deal when it came to a brand new gown that was made to order. The factory made gowns for bridal shops at that time for hundreds of dollars and even for as much as $5,000. Neither Mom nor Pop complained much about the price.

The gown was gorgeous. You should see the photos.

Mom was more generous with my gown than Mrs. Cohen had been with Frieda's. Sydelle wore my gown after I did. Sydelle, however, was a little shorter than I and a little more generously built. The dress had to be taken up and the seams let out. The following January, my skinny cousin Shirley wore it to her wedding. The dress had to be taken up just a little but the seams had to be taken in all of the way. Petite, plump cousin Milly was next. The hem went all of the way up and the seams all of the way out.

After that, my gown had lost its elegance and had become a *shmattah.* Mom kept it stored in the basement in case somebody else wanted to use it. Nobody did. Nobody was that desperate. After a while the gown became moldy and had to be thrown out.

The fate of Frieda's shopworn gown, which didn't really fit her (after all, what do you expect from a bargain) was no better. Mrs. Cohen, true to her word, kept it carefully wrapped up in tissue paper for the future generation. Mrs. Cohen was prescient. Frieda and Irv had three daughters but not one of them was married in it. It, too, had become moldy and had to be thrown out.

To this day, cousin Milly loves to tell the story about my wedding gown. In time, Milly and Lou had two daughters. But by the time the girls grew up, times had changed. They would each want their own gown. Milly had cause to remember the borrowed gown with fondness.

The wedding, however, was awful. All three of our weddings were awful. The food was awful. The band was awful. Sydelle's father had an "in" with the band and they didn't charge much for all of the noise they made. And, boy, did they make noise!

But of all the weddings, ours was the worst. The rabbi came two hours late. Had it been a Saturday night it would not have been a problem. Everybody could sleep late on Sunday. But we were married on Sunday evening. By the time the rabbi came, everybody was starving and worried about getting up in time for work the next day.

The rabbi, his face radiant from happiness, was late because he had just come from his daughter's engagement party. He explained this to us while we were signing the *ketubah* and then, again, during the ceremony under the *chupah*. He forgot to say anything about us or about our getting married. Nobody smiled with him. We all looked at our watches.

Anyway, awful weddings or not, we all stayed married which goes to show. What it goes to show, I'm not sure, but it must go to show *something*.

Acknowledgements

I thank my husband, Hans Benjamin, for always being where and when I need him. I thank David Brauner for being my mentor, for his diligence, patience and encouragement. I thank our daughter, Judy for her sound advice and willingness and ability to follow through when I could not. This book would not have been finished without her. Also, my appreciation and gratitude to Eric Miller, Inge Schaeffer, Joan Knutsen, Dorothy Rosenthal and our granddaughter, Elise, for giving me their honest opinions and encouragement.

About the Author

Born and raised in New York City, Norma Marx moved to Jerusalem with her husband after raising her family and working in the Philadelphia area for several decades. During her seventeen years in Jerusalem, Norma found her voice as a short story writer. Her writing examines her own history, her life in Jerusalem, perspectives on the Muslim world; memories of Irene, a most remarkable Holocaust survivor; and works of fiction. Norma's stories are all personal, many are humorous and poignant and some are purposefully challenging. Now living in Boca Raton, Florida, Norma has had several of her stories published in her community monthly newspaper. This is her first published collection.